Praise for the 13 Reasons for Murder Series

"…hard to put down and am keen to read the next in the series."—Reader's Favorite 5-Star

"Full of sass, good friends, and a bit of blood, this novel was a joy to read."—Julie E.

"…suspenseful, addictive…hope there are more books with this character."—BookBub Review

"I look forward to…learning more about Britney."—Studiohnh.com Review

"…oddly addictive…cannot wait for the next book…"—Amazon.ca Review

"…flows at a quick pace and leaves you wanting more…" —Goodreads Review

"The plot is fresh and unique, a nice change to read something a little different…"—Reader's Favorite 4-Star

"…well written and kept me on the edge of my seat…"—Heather W.

13 Reasons for Murder Harlot

13 Reasons for Murder (#8)

Amanda Byrd

BLACKSHEEP
PRESS

Blacksheep Press, LLC

Contents

About the Author

Amanda Byrd is obsessed with fictional serial killers. From Patrick Bateman to Dr. Hannibal Lecter to Dexter Morgan and every butcher in between, Amanda loves figuring out what drives fiction's deadliest monsters. When she's not busy writing, Amanda can be found reading, playing video games, or watching shows and movies like Mindhunter, Hannibal, and Dexter. She lives in Florida with her bloodthirsty, flesh-eating cat.

Follow Amanda online: www.amandabyrd.net
Sign up for my Deadly Insiders Club and get a free story

Follow Amanda online:
Facebook: Author Amanda Byrd
Instagram: amanda_byrd_author
Goodreads: Amanda Byrd
Bookbub: Amanda Byrd

For Ben

One

I ROCKED OUT HARD as I drove.

In the future, affection will discover you
Shatter the shackles that confine you
A single evening will jog your memory
Of the moments we shared before going our distinct paths

Tears rolled down my face as I sang and banged my head like I'd never heard of whiplash. I gripped the steering wheel until my knuckles threatened to burst through the skin. My nails dug into the soft leather, then pushed it into my palms. I squeezed tighter, afraid I might lose grip from all the crying.

I stopped at the red light I could barely see, my vision was so blurred by tears and swollen eyelids.

"Fuck you!" I screamed.

The guy in the Charger next to me looked over and flipped me off. I nodded, swinging my chin up in acknowledgment. I didn't care if he thought the screaming and cursing was directed at him. It wasn't.

"Fuck you! And your love! And every good fucking memory you ever gave me!"

I bowed my head, crying harder.

"GodDAMMIT!" I slammed a fist on the gear shifter, pissed off at Dario for being him, and at the light for turning green.

I pressed the gas pedal, headed for the beach. I could cry in my Jeep there, and no one would look twice or stop to ask me if I was okay. These days, we lived in a world where people didn't do those things anymore for fear that others would even breathe on them wrong.

"I loved you so much for so long, and what did you do?" I said, the venom dripping from every syllable.

The song ended and changed to an-all-too-familiar one. One I'd listened to so many times—for weeks—after we broke up.

As dust takes flight, I leave you far from sight
A stranded soul, in ice, lost, and alone
Once out of control, with no path to stroll
You're a memory, you don't existBefore life's thread is cut, think about this
Consider me when solitude's your only kiss
I forewarned you, don't forget my words
As stitches fail and crimson rivers gush in herdsRemember me

I turned left at the light and backed in to an empty spot, turning the volume up to the limit. After shifting into park and setting the emergency brake, I continued to rock out, head banging and singing.

The song ended on "Remember me," and my voice cracked harder than it had the day I stabbed Dario in the heart.

My forehead hit the steering wheel, and I fell apart.

Two

I DIDN'T KNOW HOW much time had passed, and I wasn't sure I cared. But my phone was ringing, waking me up from my tear-induced sleep.

I looked in the mirror on the visor. My forehead had leather stitch marks embedded in it, and there was crust on my left cheek. A crust from which protein I didn't know.

My phone kept ringing, and the name that showed on the touch screen in the dash was one I'd expected to see.

I didn't answer in time to stop it from going to voice mail, and I was oddly okay with that. Under normal circumstances, I'd have raced to pick it up, but at this moment, I didn't care about anything other than my pain.

I felt bad as I lifted my left hand to look at the beautiful ring on my finger. Stu loved me, and I loved him. But something about the finality of killing Dario hurt so much more than I could have ever imagined. I swore to Stu I was over that piece of shit. Why did my heart betray me like this?

My hands, eyes, and face hurt. I couldn't go home looking like this, could I? How would Stu feel if he saw me? Would he be mad? Empathetic? Resentful? What would I tell him?

I sucked in a deep, steadying breath and returned his call.

"Hey, babe," Stu greeted.

"Hi." I sniffled.

"You okay?"

"Not really. I didn't…"

Stu was silent. Was he mad? Disappointed? Feeling betrayed?

"Brit," he started, "I need you to know I'm not mad. I know how much you cared for him. You may not have felt it recently—hell, since you broke up—but I need you to know it's okay. You'll be okay. *We* will be okay."

I sniffled the runny nose and tears back.

"Brit, come home. Please?"

I nodded for too long before realizing he couldn't see me.

"'Kay," I responded, my voice barely a whisper.

"Drive safely, please. I love you," Stu said before ending the call.

I turned the radio up.

Take your broken promisesAnd don't come back againIt's time to say bye-byeI gotta quit you where you sitTake your broken promisesIt's time to say bye-byeI gotta quit you where you sit, sitI gotta quit you where you sit

I walked through the garage door into the kitchen, where Stu sat at the table, a beer in front of him. Across the table was an open bottle of red moscato and a glass poured just below the rim. The left corner of my mouth moved upward in a tiny smirk. This man knew me better than I sometimes knew myself. How was that even possible?

I dragged my feet as I walked to my seat across from Stu, pausing before pulling the chair out. I looked at Stu and forced a smile, making my puffy, tear-streaked face sorer. He stood and wrapped his arms around me.

I crumpled into a crying heap on the floor, Stu's arms still around me. He just held me while I cried.

Gently, Stu pulled me up and walked me to the couch, where I slumped, still a mess. I managed to sit up enough to snatch the box of tissues from the coffee table. I was blowing my nose when Stu walked back in carrying the bottle and that same full glass. He set them down and went, presumably, to retrieve his beer.

When he returned, I was curled around a pillow on my side, Minion headbutting my face as I shook.

Stu sat down near my knees, on the edge of the couch, and rubbed my leg. I wanted to reach for his hand but lacked the energy to. I wanted to hug him, or even sit up to let him hold me as I felt my pain. Pain that felt so natural yet so foreign. Was I supposed to have emotions like this? Was I supposed to have emotions at all? I was a fucking *murderer*, for fuck's sake. What were these internalized things doing and why?

If he ever hurts you

True love won't betray you

You know I'll still love you

Though we embraced and went our scattered ways

"Why…fucking WHY?" I strained. My throat hurt from all the crying, but I needed to scream, or be loud, or something—anything other than be soft. "I just... AH! What's with these feelings? Why do I even have them? Killers aren't supposed to have hearts—" I buried my face in the pillow, sobbing again.

Stu lay on me, his head on the side of my waist. He rubbed my back. I didn't think it had anything to do with him not knowing what to do—he did, he even knew what to say, always. Was he simply letting me get it all out? Could I be so lucky to have a *real* human to be engaged to?

"Stu?" I mumbled into the pillow.

"Hmm?"

"What did I do to deserve a good and decent human like you?"

Stu scoffed. "Baby, I'm not the 'human' you think I am." He sat up and gently stroked my exposed cheek. "I'm the sociopath the police force needs."

Three

For a moment, my brain froze. Then, I chuckled.

"You're a mess," I joked.

"But I'm not. I can do things others can't. I can compartmentalize and detach. No one else on the force can do that. Hell, they've even started calling me Socio-officer."

I almost choked on a giggle at that, but I wasn't sure if he was being serious. The Stu Jones I knew was a kind, empathetic, caring man. He couldn't be the man he claimed to be. Could he?

"I'm serious, Brit. That's what some of them call me," he replied, half-amused.

"But why? You're kind, and decent, and empathetic…"

"For you," he swallowed. "For you I am all of those things. For them?" He took a swig of his beer. "I'm everything you'll ever read about sociopaths, though I personally lean more toward Anti-Social Personality Disorder."

I lay there, digesting what he'd just said. *Anti-Social Personality Disorder? Who was he, fucking Dah-*

mer, minus being gay and eating me? No, not my Stu. Not my sweet, sensitive Stu.

I cleared my throat. "Clarification?"

Stu took a deep breath, appearing to think about how to explain it to me—me! Of all people, me!

"I don't think it's an act, if that's where you're headed. I know I compartmentalize and detach. I leverage these things to my advantage, and they've made me successful at what I do. Could you imagine me in Criminal Investigations, Major Crimes, or Violent Crimes divisions? I'd be an asset, no doubt."

I started to ponder what he'd just said but was interrupted.

"None of this means I don't truly and genuinely love you. I do. More than anything or anyone I've ever loved before. Britney, you are my person. Nothing you could say or do could ever change that."

Wanna bet?

If I hadn't been crying already, I would have started right then. And I did. Again.

Stu inched around me and farther up the couch, lying behind me. I wrapped my arm around him as best I could, soaking in the love. He didn't feel *bad* for me; he felt *empathy*. As far as I knew, he didn't know what I was going through. He'd never killed the one person—the *only* person—he'd ever considered reproducing with. The one person who truly saw and knew the demons inside because they were shared demons. After all, I was still alive.

I wanted to speak, to say something, but I couldn't. For the first time with him, I was at a loss for words. Okay, not the first time. I was speechless when he proposed. But that was the only other time I could remember.

We lay there silent for what felt like hours. I opened my eyes and finally spoke.

"Thank you."

It was a simple sentiment, though I knew Stu would know what I meant by that without explanation.

He nodded, his cheekbone digging into my ribcage. "You're welcome."

Neither of us needed to say anything more. We understood each other on a level others could only dream of. That same level that Dario and I had once been on. It was as beautiful as it was infuriating.

Dario and I had this level of understanding—to a degree. Me and Stu? It was the entirety of our relationship, the foundation. People would kill for this. And here I was, having it twice. Sure, I'd killed the man I'd only somewhat had it with, but *twice in a lifetime* felt like cheating somehow. Or an absurd amount of luck. Not that I considered myself lucky at the moment. I'd killed Dario to spare other women from his narcissistic abuse. And here I was talking to Stu like he was my patient and I was his goddamned psychiatrist. Is this what Dr. Bedelia du Maurier felt when Hannibal Lecter talked to her? Fuck me.

I closed my eyes again, trying to regain some sense of self enough to go up to bed. Stu must have seen or sensed me, because he spoke and nudged me at the same time.

"Come on, let's get you into bed."

"But it's only 7:30," I whined after looking at the clock screensaver on the TV.

Stu began to tickle my sides lightly. I squirmed and rolled off the couch. I did try to be nimble but ended up ass down on the beer table, almost banging my knee in the process. I wanted to laugh, but all I could do was smirk half-heartedly. My heart hurt as though I'd rammed the knife into my own heart, not Dario's. We stood slowly, facing each other. Stu reached his hands out to help guide me like I was drunk.

I *felt* drunk—from exhaustion instead of alcohol. I slunk up the stairs, holding the wall with one hand, Stu's guiding hand on my hip with the other. Together, we got me undressed and under the covers. I shimmied and twisted, finally getting myself comfortable, my eyelids fluttering. Stu kissed my forehead, nose, then lips.

"Goodnight, my queen," he whispered as he stood. He'd reached the door before I stopped him.

"Can you bring me my book or Kindle, please?"

Stu chuckled. "You're half-asleep as it is."

I smiled faintly. "I know, but I feel like I need the distraction to be able to actually sleep."

He nodded, and vanished, returning shortly after, Kindle in hand.

"I figured this would be easier because it's smaller," he said handing it to me.

"Thank you." I blew him a kiss. "I love you."

"I love you, too. Now get some rest. If you decide to stay home tomorrow, I'll stay with you if you want. I understand if you want to be alone, too, so don't feel bad saying no."

"Mm," was all I could utter with the little brain power I had left.

He kissed me again, then turned back for the door.

"I'll be up in a bit. I'm going to finish my beer first," he said on his way out the door.

I didn't respond, only opened my Kindle cover and swiped the screen to unlock it. My mind wandered back into the story I'd been reading. Something about a former elite soldier exacting revenge on his team for framing and leaving him to die in the Iraqi desert. It was short, but damn was it good. I'd already wishlisted all of the books it was the backstory for, and before my eyes closed at the end of a paragraph, I single-click bought all the available books in that series.

Four

THE NEXT MORNING, I awoke to the smell of freshly brewed coffee and breakfast. My brain screamed at me to get out of bed as fast as I could, but my body screamed different things. Moving fast was not going to happen. Hell, I wasn't even sure I had any sense of coordination. This was the worst hangover I'd ever experienced. And I'd barely finished a glass of wine!

I rolled over and sat up and pulled my robe on. Attempting to stand was a fun challenge, but I pulled it off.

"Fuck me! Why does this feel worse than a tequila hangover?" I grumbled as I shuffled to the bathroom. "Stupid emotions."

Like molasses in January in a Northern state, I got myself to a somewhat presentable form: teeth and hair brushed, slippers, and robe. Not that it mattered to Stu. He loved me regardless. I just wanted to *feel* more like myself.

When I reached the living room, I looked at the clock on the TV: 7:30 a.m. I nodded, continuing my shuffle into the kitchen.

Stu was working two frying pans, one for eggs and another for bacon.

"Smells great," I commented sniffing the air.

"There's coffee ready. If I'd known you were awake, I'd have poured you some," Stu said, looking up at me as he tonged slices of crispy bacon onto a plate covered in paper towels.

I rushed to yank the paper towels from the plate just in time for him to set the grease-dripping slices down.

"Never ruin perfectly good bacon by draining the grease," I said with a smirk.

Stu nodded and kissed me.

"Good morning. How did you sleep?"

I somehow poured us both some coffee. "I don't really know," I answered blowing on mine, "I suppose that's a good thing."

Stu chuckled as he plated eggs and bacon, bringing me a plate full of both.

"You know," he started, "if you're not going in today, you should probably let Barb know." He eyed the clock on the wall above the table.

"Shit!" I ran upstairs for my phone, grabbing it and immediately calling her. That was the fastest I'd moved in a few days.

Barb answered, half-groggy.

"Brit, you're fine. I've got this," she reassured me.

"Okay, thanks, Barb," I said, trying to sound as grateful as I thought I felt. My voice wasn't very good at the acting bit, though.

I must have been that exhausted still, to not be able to act the way I usually could. Killing Dario really fucked me in so many ways. Did I still have the cold heart I once had?

Everything remains exactly as it was.

I am I, and you are you,

and the old life that we lived so fondly together is untouched, unchanged.

Whatever we were to each other, that we are still.

Call me by the old familiar name.

Speak of me in the easy way which you always used.

Put no difference into your tone.

Wear no forced air of solemnity or sorrow.

The song had started playing in my head as I hung up the phone. Before, even. Fuck me. I didn't want to go back to the girl I was so long ago, but this was the only way I knew to handle the pain.

I'd known since our first fight—mine and Dario's—that I'd be the villain of our story. And I'd been more than okay with that. It was the way things had to be, and I was more than good at being that villain.

But FUCK! It hurt anyway. I never expected to feel the level of pain I currently felt. Ever. For anyone or anything. I was a cold-blooded killer, for fuck's sake. Who was I to have *actual* feelings?

I plopped down on the floor, not even aiming for the bed, and sobbed. I wished, when I could breathe again, that I couldn't feel anything ever again. Then my brain would pipe up with, "If you didn't feel any-thing ever again, you couldn't continue to love Stu. Or allow him to love you."

Fucking brain, asshole.

It wasn't wrong. It was 120 percent correct. If I didn't—or couldn't—feel things, I wouldn't be in love with Stu. At all.

I closed my eyes. *The safety of disbelief.* I didn't know what it was but…I did. I knew that Dario was broken and couldn't be what I wanted or needed him to be—because he wasn't willing to look in the mirror.

The safety of disbelief was that I believed he could be the man he swore he *wanted* to be. The truth was knowing he never actually would be. The safety in that wasn't something *I* was ever willing to see. And then I did. And I killed him. Because he was a true piece of shit.

Stu? Stu *knew* what and who he was. I envied that. Particularly now, when I was doubting those things about myself.

And then—then I was back there. Still feeling things for Dario. Things I didn't want to feel for him. Things I shouldn't still be feeling for him. Yet there they were. And I hated—abhorred—every second of it.

Five

A WEEK OR SO had gone by with me in a haze. I was a robot on autopilot. Not much registered in that time frame, if anything at all. I moved and did things like work, but I didn't remember any of it.

I was working in my office one afternoon when a knock on the doorframe pulled me from the monotony.

"Barb, just—"

I looked up and saw the man I'd been afraid to talk to about any of this. He closed the door, strolled to the chair across the desk from me, and sat.

I swallowed so hard, I was sure he'd heard it.

"Britney," he started, "I don't know what's been going on with you, but I'm worried. Are you okay?"

I stared at him like he was stupid, like he should've known what had gone on. But he didn't because how could he? I hadn't told him, and Stu wouldn't say a word without talking to me first.

"Joe, I-I—" I broke off. I had no words that could speak the volume of my heart and mind. Then it came to me. "I had a nervous breakdown. I've been doing too much, apparently. I'm under great psychiatric care." I chuckled in spite of myself.

It wasn't a total lie. I did have a great therapist in Ben.

Joe nodded.

"I've been worried. I haven't heard from you in over a week. I'm glad to hear you're on the mend." He smiled, that big, friendly, warm smile he had.

On the mend, right. If that's what you think, keep thinking it.

And then I said something I probably shouldn't have.

"Joe, look, I'm really busy. I've been out for over a week and need to get caught up. Can I call you in a couple days?"

I stood and walked around my desk. Joe stood as I got closer, knowing I was kicking him out without saying the words. I hugged him.

"Thank you." I wrapped my arms around him in a hug. "It means a lot that you came here looking for me, and that you care."

"I'm only channeling my inner Britney," he said with a hearty chuckle. I giggled a bit, fighting back my impression of my namesake, but I couldn't hold it, appropriate or not.

"It's Britney, bitch."

Joe let out a belly laugh.

"Only you, kid. Only you." He pushed me back to arm's length, keeping his hands on my arms. "You're stronger than anyone I've met, and that's a lot of people. But you… Kid, you're something else. I don't know how you do it, but I admire you for it."

You don't want to know.

"Thanks, Joe. I appreciate that. I don't feel it much yet, but I'll be back to myself soon. And when I am, you'll be the first person I call."

Joe nodded and saw himself out as I walked back behind my desk.

When I sat down, I had no energy left. So I did what I needed to: I finished the email I was typing when Joe had come in, hit Send, and called it a day. I didn't bother to look at the clock on my monitor as I shut down. I didn't care.

What I cared about was dead. By my hands. And he deserved every bit of it. The other person I cared about was working until ten o'clock tonight. The fuzzy person I loved more than anything in this world, was at home, sleeping or tearing shit up. I never knew until I got home. *Maybe I should get cameras?*

I packed up and on my way out the door let Barb know I'd be working from home tomorrow.

"Everything okay?" she asked.

"Yeah, I'm just out of energy. If I'm up to it, I'll come in, but if I don't, you know how to reach me. And yes, I'll be working, even if I go to the beach," I joked.

Not that working from some tiki bar or restaurant on the beach was a bad idea. It's not like my laptop wasn't one of the more expensive ones and everything wasn't backed up to the cloud.

I drove home in the same brain fog I'd been in for over a week. Would this ever end?

When I walked into the house, Minion greeted me in the kitchen. I dropped my things on a chair at the table and scooped her up, hugging her close. I lost it all over again. What was wrong with me? I hadn't cried in a week, but I was now? Something wasn't right, wasn't normal. Was I? Was what I was feeling, this emotional roller coaster, normal? I pulled out my phone and used the trusty Google machine, typing in my "symptoms" as it were.

"Huh," I said aloud. "Grief."

I shrugged and set the phone down on the table as I walked to the refrigerator. Pulling out the bottle of local-made wine, I debated using some kind of drinking apparatus instead of chugging straight from the bottle. The glass won, and I wasn't entirely sure why.

As I turned the corner and placed my foot on the first stair, I heard the door unlock. *Why the fuck don't you carry on your person, Britney?*

It would have been too obvious if I went plowing up the stairs to grab one of my guns, so as the door-knob twisted, I chugged the wine. *Not the best idea.* Then I broke the glass from the stem, making a fine weapon for stabby purposes.

I raised my arm, poised to attack.

Six

STU WAS LOOKING DOWN as he walked through the entryway. I was still standing there, pointy wine glass stem ready to stab. As he looked up, I didn't bother shifting the broken glass to play it off. It wasn't worth the lies. Besides, he never judged me, and he sure as shit wouldn't start now.

Stu chuckled.

"Babe, what are you doing? Are you okay?"

I dropped my arm, twisting the broken glass so the pointy end wouldn't actually stab him, and walked over to him.

"No, I don't think I am. I'm sad again," I answered, flopping down on a stair and bursting into tears for the who-knew-how-manyeth time.

Stu came over and sat with me, his arm around my shoulders.

"Brit, it's called grief, and it's normal. Please don't be so hard on yourself," he cooed.

"I'm not me anymore, am I?" I asked him as I picked my head up to look him in the eyes. I faltered, dropping my eyes to his lips so he'd at least think I was looking at him.

He gingerly placed a finger under my chin, tilted my head up so I *had* to look him in the eyes.

"I love you. I'm here for you. No matter what, okay? I wouldn't have proposed if I only wanted to judge you and manipulate you like he did. I am not him. You know that deep in your heart. Me being different from anyone you've ever met is why you said yes. You don't judge me, and I don't judge you. We're the same, and you feel that in your bones. Know how I know?"

I raised an eyebrow, in a sort of disbelief that he was saying these things.

"Because you talk in your sleep." He let out the tiniest of giggles then.

I pulled back, in shock, but half laughing. I shoved him playfully.

"You're so full of shit," I said.

"I'm serious! You do. And you talk about me… and Dario. You're going through grief, babe. And I'm not upset or mad about it. You may not have been with him long, but you've gotta admit that he fucked you up. Even if you only ever admit it to yourself. That's how you'll get through this. And I'm here for you always," he said. "But I have to ask, why were you about to stab me?"

In my delirium, I burst out laughing.

"Because I'm paranoid and thought you were someone trying to break in." Stu nodded.

"You realize John Sweet is still in jail, right?"

"For now," I muttered.

"And if I have anything to say about it—"

"There's nothing you can do. It was only a break-in," I said.

"That doesn't mean we can't extend the restraining order," Stu replied as if I hadn't just cut him off.

"Fair enough, but you basically live here now, too. I don't think he's that stupid."

"Well, he did break in and get himself shot by you. This is Florida. Everyone has a gun. So yeah, he's stupid."

We both chuckled.

"Touché," I said.

I nuzzled his shoulder with my face and let my cheek rest there for a few minutes. *Do I really deserve this man? Do I deserve anyone this good? Granted, he's admitted he's also a psychopath of sorts. Wait one fucking minute...*

"Babe?"

"Hm?""You told me you're the sociopath the force needs..."

"I did. What about it?"

"Well, you're capable of empathy and love, so that automatically cancels you out of psychopathy." I said it with such a finality of my tone, Stu was forced back a little bit.

"That's true," he replied, contemplative. "So I'm not a psychopath by definition of the DSM-5, but I am, in fact, a psychopath. Some of us lower on the scale are actually capable of such things."

"You sound like a shrink," I observed with a half-hearted giggle.

"I should. I've seen enough of them in my life," he said dryly.

"Tell me more?"

"Only if we can go sit on the couch."

"Deal!"

Stu stood and helped me up. On our walk six feet away, I stopped, confused.

"Hang on. Why are you even home? Aren't you working until 10 p.m.?"

Stu nodded and smiled. "I'm on lunch, so it'll have to be a condensed version for now."

I nodded, continuing to walk.

When we sat down, he started telling me about his early twenties, and how he thought something was off. He'd decided going to a therapist and opening up would help. That therapist referred him to a psychiatrist for diagnosis. And that started the search for the right combination of psychiatrist and therapist for him.

"It takes a while, kinda like finding the right meds for depression," he said.

I nodded, having known plenty of people on antidepressants.

He continued for another twenty or so minutes, giving me a brief rundown of just how many shrinks he'd seen until he found the one he was currently seeing.

"But…you're not on meds, so why keep seeing a shrink?" I asked.

"He taught me how to control it without them," he replied as if it were a simple thing.

"Oh."

"I promise to tell you more about it later. For now, I've got to get back on patrol." He kissed me deeply and stood.

I followed, kissing him one more time as he walked out.

"Be safe," I said. It carried the same weight as "I love you" did when your first responder was on duty.

"I will," he said before closing the door.

Somehow, I felt better and didn't know why. Was my grief finally starting to let up? I decided not to dwell on it and locked the door before going upstairs to change.

When I came back down, I turned on *Hannibal* the movie, zoned out, and passed out.

Seven

Six weeks later, I was feeling better. So much better that I'd pulled in three new contracts for temps. I was on a roll. And then Katie walked in.

Barb was out for the day, owing to throwing up for the past two days. Even I knew what that meant, but she went to the doctor anyway instead of buying a home test. She was like that.

"Hey there!" I greeted. "I'll be right with you. Make yourself as comfortable as you can. I just have to finish this paragraph."

"Sure," the feminine-yet-masculine, super bitchy voice responded.

Great, she's one of those.

I decided to finish the proposal that was requested by the newest legal team in the city. They were a sizable team, too. Each lawyer had two to three assistants who performed various jobs; they were a team of about forty and needed temp and temp-to-permanent hires. They came to me via Joe Osten. That man...

I completed the proposal and sent it to Julie for proofreading and editing before walking into the reception area.

"Sorry about that," I said, "I'm Britney." I stuck my hand out to this grumpy brunette.

She stayed seated, eying my hand as though it carried every deadly disease in the book. *If this bitch only knew.*

"I'm Katie," she responded without offering her hand back. "I'm a laid-off teacher and desperate."

"Well, it would behoove you to shake my hand then," I said with slight menace, "I'm the biggest temp agency in the city, soon to be tri-county area. And manners are expected of people I send anywhere."

Katie cleared her throat and stood, nodding.

"Apologies. I'm just frustrated that it's gotten this far."

She still hadn't tried to be polite back. Who the fuck did she think she was?

"I respect that, but you still are incapable of being polite, even after being told it's expected. Katie, was it? Look, I want to help you. People like you are why I started this company. But *you* specifically... Well, I just don't think you're a fit. Have a good day," I said before spinning on my heel.

I'd made it about four steps back toward my office before she spoke.

"Please. I'm desperate."

I didn't bother to look back at her.

"Your attitude shows me the truth. Have a great day," I said, closing my office door to make a point.

The main door dinged her exit, and I continued working.

I'd been feeling like myself again and had talked to Ben numerous times in the past six weeks to get me to this point. He'd warned me the grief would continue in cycles until it just sort of disappeared. I might have moments of sadness here and there, but the worst was over. And if I continued to see him and go to my grief group, I'd be right as rain. So, that was my plan: continue until I didn't need to anymore.

My thoughts drifted back to Katie. Who the fuck did she think she was? She was completely incapable of even remaining professional. She clearly needed a job, and I'd gotten good at spotting narcissists, and she absolutely was one. There was no mistaking that.

What struck me the most, though, was that she couldn't even put her mask on for me. What did that mean? Did it even matter? I decided it didn't, and if she showed back up, I *might* be kind. It wasn't like I hadn't found myself in tight spots in the past.

She must have heard my thoughts because I didn't hear the door ding, but I recognized her voice.

"Miss Cage? Are you here?" she called.

I didn't respond because I wanted to hear what she had to say to my still-closed door that she couldn't say to my face.

"I'm sorry. It was very unprofessional and rude of me to behave that way earlier." *If this didn't sound familiar…*

I chose to remain silent. I wanted to see how far I could get her to go. Masochism? Maybe. It sounded so familiar. But I held strong. Maybe the grief was really gone.

"Miss Cage, please. I'm currently substitute teaching, and it's barely enough. I need something else." She paused. "And you're being rather unkind."

There it was. The beginning of the blame-shifting. And did I hear an English accent? Weird. The Brits I knew were straightforward, but not in the same way. More "normal."

I rose from my chair, silently stalking toward the closed door, careful not to make any noise.

"You're being unreasonable," she continued.

I opened the door and scoffed in her face.

"That's no way to win anyone over," I commented. She nodded.

"I understand that. But I'm desperate," she reiterated.

This fucking cunt thinks she can manipulate me? HA! I'd been fucked over by one of the best. She won't get to me. Or maybe she could in a different way. In my mind, I rubbed my hands together like an animated movie villain.

"Still not winning me over," I said flatly, crossing my arms over my chest.

She nodded again, still refusing to accept responsibility.

"Please? I need your help."

Getting closer to her could be beneficial. I still haven't chosen my next kill, and I've got that itch again...

I changed tack and told her to sit at one of the applicant computers. She filled out all the necessary paperwork, and I told her I'd call her in a day or two. She acted as grateful as she was capable of.

I'd decided to try to lure her into being as close to a friend as she could be.

My next kill was cemented.

Eight

STU WAS MAKING DINNER when I walked in.

"How was work, babe?" He asked.

I cackled.

"Sounds like you're back to you," he muttered, stirring the soup.

"Let me tell you about this woman," I said, pouring a glass of wine. "Want a beer?"

He lifted an almost-empty bottle. I grabbed a fresh one from the fridge. I kissed him on the cheek as I popped the top off and set it on the counter, swapping it for the now-empty one.

I stood next to him as he stirred and added spices, telling him about Katie. He agreed that I needed to befriend this woman for my own reasons. The world would be much better off without her. Especially the kids she taught.

"If she's like this with adults, can you imagine how she is with children?" Stu observed.

I shuddered visibly.

"If I had, or wanted, kids, she wouldn't be their teacher," I replied, knowing his question was rhetorical.

I took a sip of wine and realized I actually sort of had a kid. I snatched my phone from my purse and called Julie. She answered in two rings.

"Hey, Brit!"

"Jules, I have a weird question for you. Did Brian ever have a teacher by the name of Katie van-some-thing?"

Silence.

"Jules?"

She sighed.

"Yes. She was awful. I'm glad they laid her off in their last round," she replied.

Oh good!

"Tell me how awful."

"Why? Brit, is everything okay?"

I explained to Julie why I needed to know, and she happily divulged everything she knew. Twenty minutes later, I was satisfied.

"Thanks, Julie."

I hung up the phone and launched into what Julie had told me about Katie. I filed him in on her being disrespectful to parents of middle schoolers, and the students themselves, often making the kids doubt their own reality. And they were too young to under-stand people like her roamed the earth. I didn't finish until Stu had set the bowls full of soup on the table and we'd sat down.

"Interesting," he commented. "So, what are you going to do?"

"I'm going to befriend her after placing her."

"Are you sure that's a good idea given how fresh everything else is?"

I clenched my teeth and swallowed.

"I am not glass. I will not shatter into a million pieces."

The venom from those words burned the table.

We ate in silence for a while.

"I'm sorry," I blurted.

"No, it's my fault. I'm sorry. That was out of line," Stu said.

I accepted that gracefully, realizing I'd fallen back into old patterns of Dario and needing to apologize for everything *I'd* said or felt.

I continued, silent once again.

"Babe—" Stu started.

"No, I get it. I fell back into that pattern. It's a hard habit to break, apparently. Even though I'd broken it a long time ago..." I looked beyond him at the wall, though I wasn't seeing the wall.

He nodded and finished his food.

We cleared the table and put the dirty dishes in the dishwasher. After he closed it, I hugged him.

"Thank you for being you," I said, wrapping my arms around the back of his neck.

I kissed him for a long time before pulling back to look him in the eyes.

"What?"

I smirked.

"Nothing." I shook my head. "Okay, that's a lie. I appreciate you so much," I said before kissing him again.

Stu smiled and pulled back, a look of realization on his face. Now it was my turn.

"What?"

"I never finished telling you about the shrinks and what all I've been through to know I'm a psychopath," he said simply.

"Is that all?" I asked with a snicker.

"Ha-ha," he mocked, grabbing another beer from the fridge then pouring me a glass of wine. "Come on, it's story time."

He had that sparkle in his eye I'd only seen when he told me he loved me. He carried both drinks to the couch, and we sat down. He took a swig of beer, then raised his bottle in toast.

"To us," he said like it was an anniversary or special occasion.

It *was* a special occasion, though. He was opening up to me like I suspected he never had to anyone else aside from his shrink.

For the next two hours, Stu told me about the dark thoughts that led him to seek out psychiatric help in the first place. They were the same as mine. The only differences being that I killed and continued to. He'd stopped to become a cop. He'd sublimated those feelings. He'd wanted to do things differently.

"I realized if I did things by the book and on the right side of the law, I could affect something greater," he said, finishing his story.

"But"—I hesitated for a moment— "was there a triggering event for you? There wasn't one for me, so..." I shrugged as I trailed off. I didn't know how to explain that, for me, killing was second nature with nothing happening to me like *Dexter* had happen to him. "Born in blood" they'd said in the books and TV show.

"Like you, I didn't really have one, either," Stu replied. "I just felt different. I *knew* I wasn't the same as other people."

I looked at him, seeing him, but he was blurry. I suddenly felt alone. I wasn't, but I felt that way. We were two psychopaths in one house. Both running around and within the laws of convention and society—federal, local, and state. We were far outside the laws of civilized humanity.

I snickered, the self-deprecating and spiteful kind of snicker.

"Different. That's one way to explain it."

We finished our drinks with a milder conversation, my statement having told Stu that was the end of the deep shit for now. Maybe for a longer period of time.

Nine

I DIALED THE PHONE number on the application.

"Hullo?" She answered with that attitude.

"Katie? Hi, it's Britney Cage at Passing Through Temp Agency. I wanted to personally call you about the offer I've got for you."

I heard her snort on the other end and fought the disdain and urge to reach through the phone and rip her throat out with my bare hands. Then I fought the scene in my head…

"So, there are two of them. One is at a publisher, temp-to-perm, pays twenty-five an hour, benefits ninety days after going permanent. The other is for a new law firm doing research, pays thirty an hour for either temp or temp-to-perm, with benefits thirty days after going permanent if that's what you choose."

There was silence on the other end. I figured she was weighing her options, that she'd hoped to go back to teaching full time but knew there was a fat chance of that happening.

"Law firm research," she stated snidely.

It took all my strength not to verbally rip her to shreds. I forced myself to remember what a cocky asshole I'd been when I was desperate, but I also had learned how to play the game. She clearly had not and apparently had no interest. Lucky for her, honestly.

I sometimes wished I weren't the bigger person. I sometimes wished I weren't the me I was. But if I weren't, I'd end up behind bars for all those murders…unable to continue making the world a better place for everyone else.

There were things I couldn't—wouldn't—let slide. This cunt's attitude was one of them. She'd get what was coming to her soon enough. I needed to hold it back long enough to somehow befriend her so it wouldn't look weird when we "hung out." Sure, the cops might come to me first. Or they wouldn't. That was of no concern to me. Besides, it wasn't like my "psychopathic" cop fiancé couldn't help in some way.

"Great," I replied. "I'll put you on the list for temp-to-perm.""Thanks," she snorted.

"Sure thing. They'll be in touch to schedule your interview. Let me know how it goes. If by some chance it doesn't work out, I can still place you with the publisher."

"Sure." She sounded distant. Or maybe she simply didn't care one way or the other. I wasn't going to bother myself trying to figure her out. I'd seen enough to know she thought she was God's gift. Textbook grandiose narcissism.

As dust takes flight, I leave you far from sight
A stranded soul, in ice, lost, and alone
Once out of control, with no path to stroll
Paralyzed, lost, and cold…

We said our goodbyes, and I needed to jog the anger out. I was working from home, so it was easy to go upstairs and change. Minion eyed me lazily from the bed as I changed.

"Disturbing the princess's sleep?" I asked her before kissing her tiny head and jogging down the stairs and out the door.

I woke up moaning and sweating. I was tangled in the comforter and struggled to unwrap myself. I twisted, turned, pulled, and yanked until…

SLAM!

Stu sat upright, gun in hand. He looked where I should have been—next to him in bed—and called out, deftly sliding out of bed.

"Brit? Where are you? Are you okay?"

I struggled a little more to get out of the blanket before answering.

"Yeah. Nightmare…" I responded, hoarse.

He came over to me and knelt by my side, helping me free myself from the soft fabric prison I was still stuck in.

"Wanna talk about it?"

I shrugged, unsure if I even remembered enough to talk about at this point.

He finally freed me, and I just sat there on the floor, naked. Staring into the void that formed in the wall. Stu leaned up against the bed next to me, his hand on my thigh, not speaking.

This—this was what someone did who truly accepted you for all you were. Like in a rom-com. This was the true love I'd always called unrealistic because I'd only ever experienced it by watching movies.

My mother is no longer in my life because of the things she put me through growing up. Dario was no longer in anyone's life because I was the universe's last straw. I need to talk to Ben about this… Could my mother be the reason why I did what I did? According to all the textbooks and DSM-5, yes. Her abuse was precisely why I was who—and what—I was.

I stood without a word, wrapped the comforter around my body like a towel, and walked out of the room. Stu put his gun back in the nightstand and followed.

We walked into the kitchen, still in silence. I opened the fridge, pulled out a beer for him, and slid it across the tabletop. Then I walked to the counter, where the bottle of moscato sat and uncorked it.

I sat at the table and clinked the neck of his bottle.

"Fuck the glass," was my phrase of choice at that moment. I chugged until I couldn't anymore, downing half the bottle.

Stu took in a healthy gulp of his beer, still choosing to say nothing.

"I-it—" I shook my head and chugged again, less this time. "Dario was in it. Standing over me as I slept. I don't think it was a night terror since I didn't freeze or anything; I could still move. It was my heavy breathing and sweat that woke me up."

Stu reached his hand across the table and put it on mine, wrapped as much around the wine bottle as it could be. He didn't need to say anything for me to understand. He was here, good and bad and all that crap that was recited in wedding vows. I didn't know what I did to deserve him, but, fuck, was I grateful for him.

"I love you," I said before finishing the bottle. "Now, let's go back to bed. Five a.m. comes quick."

Ten

A WEEK OR SO later, I felt a lot better. Not loads, but enough to be able to focus on things again like I could before the nightmare. Maybe that old adage about time healing all wounds was true. That song I had been hearing over and over in my head had started to fade, too.

"Fuck that guy," I caught myself mumbling.

I was at the office that I increasingly found myself wondering why I owned. In a time when every other company had remote everything, why was I one of the holdouts? What sense did it make for me? Applicants, sure, but for me? Barb was more than capable of running the place without me. But I was locked into a lease I sure as shit didn't want to buy out of. Maybe I'd work from home? No. I didn't have a Wawa across the street. Or a Starbucks. Though I could work from home most days… I decided to give it more thought. It wouldn't reduce my overhead, though.

We weren't even close to a recession or financial instability in any way as a country. Not yet, at least. But I found myself thinking of ways to save the company money. Was capitalism so bad? My temps were compensated much better than other agencies offered—I started my people at twenty dollars an hour minimum.

Were these thoughts merely a distraction from my own feelings about life?

I shook my head, quickly getting back to work on the proposal I had been drafting. Then my computer dinged.

You have a visitor, I read as my office door opened.

I looked up to see Stu walking in with a bouquet of flowers. A smile spread across my face.

"What's this for?" I asked, standing.

He handed me the flowers.

"I love you and wanted to show you how much I appreciate you. Is that not reason enough?"

I grinned, not having a proper response.

"But why bring them here? I don't know that I'll be here for the next week," I said.

Stu's face screwed up in confusion.

"Where are you going?" He asked, his offense clear.

"Home. I'll be working from home," I stated.

Stu relaxed; his posture returned to normal.

I giggled and wrapped my arms around his neck, embracing him as only a lover could.

"Thank you," I said before I kissed him.

We'd just finished dinner and I was loading the dishwasher when Stu came up from behind me, almost catching a steak knife to the neck.

He backed up, hands up as though he was a criminal being drawn down on.

"Whoa!"

I shook my head.

"I…sorry. I…have no idea why I did that," I admitted, hanging my head and tossing the knife into the dishwasher.

"You're fine," he said. "Promise."

I merely nodded, accepting that, even though I didn't.

We finished cleaning up, and Stu poured me another glass of wine. Then he grabbed a beer from the fridge, snickering as he sat down.

"Most people would think we're alcoholics," he half joked.

"Fuck them." I said, raising my glass. "They don't know us or our lives or that we're, in fact, *not*."

Stu tapped his bottle against my glass in agreement.

"Amen," he replied before taking a healthy swig.

"Tell me something," I implored after swallowing a hefty amount of wine.

Stu arched an eyebrow at me.

"Your childhood," I said matter-of-factly. "I want to know about all of it."

Stu stared at me, unblinking. I stared right back, indicating I wasn't joking.

He took his time, obviously internally debating what he should tell me.

"*All* of it," I reiterated.

"That's a heavy load for tonight. I'll tell you some of it tonight and the rest another night," he said.

"Fair enough," I replied.

Stu sat silent for a few minutes, perhaps thinking where to start. Then, he told me the first thing he could remember, a traumatic incident with his mother. She beat the ever-living shit out of him at the age of three. It didn't get any better from there. It got to a point where she didn't just beat him but abused him in other ways, physically, emotionally, and mentally.

I understood the mental and emotional abuse—my mother had done the same. But the physical abuse he'd endured made me cry. He noticed and finished the story he'd been telling.

"This"—he pointed at me with his bottle— "is why I said it's too much for one night."

I nodded solemnly.

"I never doubted you," I mumbled, a cry caught in my throat.

"You asked," Stu snorted.

"And you shared, so don't take it out on me."

He simply nodded, understanding he was in the wrong on this. Sure, I'd asked. But he'd obliged. He knew we couldn't *truly* understand each other without telling me these things. He didn't have to like it. Hell, I didn't like sharing with my traumas just as much. And here I was, trauma dumping for how long now?

"I'm sorry for what happened to you," I said, looking him in the eyes.

Stu just looked back into mine, leaving me to decipher the meaning behind the shade change. A challenge I met head on because I wanted to know. He was clearly frustrated, and his eyes did not belie that. There was something else in them, though. Love. This was what true love looked like. The ability to bare all and be deeply intimate.

He stood from his seat, tossed the now-empty bottle, and poured a glass of water.

"I think I'm headed to the couch," he said.

"Want some company?"

He nodded, barely able to look me in the face now.

I stood, took his hand, and led the way.

Eleven

Stu took some time to digest that he'd let me that far in. Into his mind and heart. I supposed he'd never expected to, which may have been fine if I were someone else. But I wasn't. I was me—his fiancée—and loved the fuck out of him. I didn't just want to know. I needed to. So I didn't bother pushing further. I knew he'd finish his story when he was ready.

Finish was exactly what he did. Two weeks had passed since that conversation. A somewhat long two weeks, fraught with tension. Until tonight.

I'd been cooking dinner when Stu walked in, uniform pants on, top unbuttoned revealing his bulletproof vest. He set his duffel down at the bottom of the stairs before coming into the kitchen and giving me a quick peck on the cheek.

"Well, hello to you, too," I said with a grin, turning my head to face him.

He was at the fridge, his back to me, plucking a beer from the shelf. When he turned around, he launched into the rest of his life, without warning.

By the time he finished, dinner was on plates in front of each of us, though neither of us had the stomach for it.

I watched Stu, playing with his food like a child would, trying to read him. It didn't last long because he looked up at me, and I found myself shying away. This man had been through so much, yet here he was, protecting the innocent the best way he knew how.

I walked around the table to him and wrapped him in a hug—the best medicine I knew of. He put a hand on my elbow, accepting as much of the hug as he could. I stepped back, knowing time was up, and began clearing the table.

"We didn't even touch the beautiful meal you made," Stu whined.

"It'll reheat all right," I said, shrugging as I picked up my plate.

By the time I was finished putting everything into containers and in the fridge, Stu had finished loading the dishwasher. I sighed, pouring the remainder of the bottle of moscato into a glass. I sighed harder when I realized I'd need to open another to make myself tired. So I did.

Stu had grabbed himself two beers and let me know he was going to pick out a movie for us to watch. I was in a bit of a fog, and shrugged.

Who was I to even be in this fog? He'd just spilled all the dark details of his childhood, and *I* was the one in a fog? How?

I wandered out to the couch and plopped beside Stu. He wrapped an arm around me and pressed Play. It was a movie we could either zone out to or fall asleep; it didn't matter. We loved this version of the movie, remake or not, and had seen it so many times. Rob Zombie had done a good job on this one, regardless of what my friends thought.

I laid my head in the nook of his shoulder and chest, fitting perfectly, and kissed his neck before settling in.

We hadn't gotten ten minutes in when Stu tapped me, signaling he needed to sit up for another beer. I took the opportunity to gulp the remaining mouthful in my glass and poured more. Neither one of us had seemed the least bit groggy enough to call it a night.

I was worried. Worried about the hit our sex life had taken, but more worried about the boxes Stu had reopened in his mind because I'd asked him to. Would he be okay?

"Babe," I started, "I'm concerned about you. I asked you to open up, and you did. But now you seem to be in this dark place, and I can't help but feel responsible for putting you back there."

Stu shook his head.

"It's not your fault. It's theirs," he said before taking another swig. "But this trauma... What you've been through… Don't you see why I love you so much?"

I was taken aback at that comment. Was he saying he felt comfortable with me?

What the fuck else could he be implying, Britney? I admonished myself. I was right, of course. That's exactly what he was saying—without saying it plainly.

He turned to face me.

"What we've both been through…the traumas and being treated like less than dirt? That we've endured on our own for so long. I can trust you with all of mine, and you can trust me with yours. How many times do you think someone gets that in their life, without being shit on again?"

I gulped audibly. He wasn't mad or irrational. He was asking a rhetorical question that we both knew the answer to. We wouldn't be engaged if I couldn't tell the difference.

"I see you," I mumbled. I didn't realize I'd said it aloud until Stu made a noise.

"You do," he followed up. "If I didn't think you did, I would never have proposed."

I raised my glass to his bottle and clinked.

"Here, here!"

It was all I could think of at that moment. Stu chuckled.

"Glad you're back to you," he said, grinning.

I wasn't sure how to react to that, so I didn't. I just drank what was left in my glass. Then, I got up thinking to grab the bottle, or what was left of it. Instead, Stu stood, knowing.

"I'll get it," he said, shaking his own bottles. "I need more, too."

While he was gone, I sat wondering. How could I mean that much to anyone? I'd never even meant that much to the woman who'd given birth to me. On the contrary, that woman *hated* me. I'd never understood that, but being in therapy with Ben helped me to at least grasp the idea that narcissists were, in fact, capable of *hating* their offspring.

I was lost in realizing how much Stu trusted and loved me when he walked back in, a look of confused horror on his face.

"The patio door is open," he said, setting the bottles down on the coffee table. "Did you do that?"

Twelve

"I'M SORRY, THE FUCKING WHAT?" I just about screamed.

"Yeah, the patio door is open. I don't remember you—"

I launched from the couch before the sentence finished, angry. Was Sweet out? No, couldn't be. At least not yet. And did I? Did I open the door to let Minion out and just not remember?

I started mumbling aloud.

"I opened the door just a little bit when I started cooking, just so it would go out instead of linger… Then I made dinner…" I was physically retracing my steps.

I sighed heavily.

"It was me. I opened the door before starting dinner," I said, looking down at my feet.

"OK."

It was all Stu could say. Usually, he had some witty retort, but after all that he'd expelled, I couldn't blame him for being unable to make fun of anything, let alone me.

He sat back down, drinking simultaneously. I watched in a form of awe; I could never do that without spilling.

Stu pressed Play on the movie, and we moved right back into the places we were before, my head in the crook of his chest and shoulder, his arm around me. I smiled and closed my eyes.

The next thing I knew, morning was streaming in through the curtains. I sat up, wiping the drool from my chin, tapping, then smacking Stu's shoulder.

"Babe. Babe. Babe," I started, "BABE! It's seven a.m.!"

Stu sat up groggily. We were still on the couch. "And?"

"Don't you… Aren't you late?"

He shook his head.

"No. If I had to be in this early, do you think I'd have had nine beers last night?"

Nine? NINE! Holy fuck, how did I not see that?

"I didn't realize…" I trailed off. "Wait. Nine? For real?"

I'd had a bottle and a half of wine on an empty stomach, and he'd polished off nine beers and *I didn't notice*? Fuck. *You're a great spouse-in-training, huh, Britney?*

As if he knew the argument in my head, Stu put a hand on my shoulder.

"You were caught up in your head. Please don't think you're awful for it. I laid a lot on you," Stu said. "Let's go to bed."

I nodded.

"Let me text Barb and let her know I'll be late," I mumbled.

"But you work from home?"

I nodded.

"Yes, but she still—Ah, fuck it. I own the place. If I'm not available, so be it. For today anyway."

We stood and went to the bedroom, disrobing on our way up the stairs. I sat on the bed to take my shorts off, and Stu kissed me. *Sex life is back*, I thought, knowing from the way he kissed me that he felt much better.

We made love for another hour, each of us reaching climax more than once before retiring to regain our energy.

"Go hard or go home," I said to Julie.

She chuckled.

"I mean it. Anything worth having is worth going hard for," I said wearing a smile.

She looked at me, knowing I was dead serious. I meant those words with every fiber of my being.

"I get that but—"

"No buts, Jules. Do it."

"But…I can't just—"

"Yes. You *can* just," I poked at her. "You *can* just write that contract. Know how I know, aside from me being the owner of this company?"

Julie cocked her head to the side, that all-telling "how" question sprawled across her face.

"Because I'm the owner of this company," I replied, "Also because I would never have put you in a position I didn't think you could handle. Now, finish typing," I said, hovering over her shoulder.

Julie laughed.

"I never would have called you if I thought you'd stand here over me," she said.

"Learned something new," I quipped.

She smiled, turning back to her monitor, typing away furiously. In less than three minutes, she was done, standing from her chair, beckoning me to sit and review her work.

I sat, reading as I did.

I took me all of three minutes to read the contract over. Jules had done an impeccable job at copying my style, though it *was* as professional as professional could get. It was a contract, after all, not an email that needed voice.

I high-fived her. Not for getting it right, but for getting it right when she thought she couldn't.

"You really need to stop letting me intimidate you," I joked. "Seriously, you're great at this. Please stop being so judgmental of yourself."

Jule blushed and said nothing. I smiled because I knew she'd be too shy to.

I stood, wrapping her in a hug, and whispered.

"You are so much more than you give yourself credit for. OWN IT."

I pulled back maybe because I wanted to see the look on her face, maybe because I wanted to see the recognition in her eyes. I got both. *Right again, or should I say as usual?*

Julie took her chair back, sitting and speaking at the same time.

"I just… You're working from home now? But you already have the office. Why not go in?"

I shrugged.

"Because I don't need to be there to work," I replied. Then I shrugged. "Besides, we're getting a new app for phone calls. It'll save me a shit ton over the landline bill."

Julie's face paled; she looked in shock.

"As long as we have internet, we're fine. And, if you really want to, you can put the app on your phone," I said, not thinking anything of it.

"I don't—I don't understand," she commented.

"Hm?" I half asked.

"You're going to teach me how to use this internet phone, right?"

I almost burst into laughter. She was much younger than me, and *she* wanted *me* to teach her how to use new technology? HA! I was a dinosaur next to her—ten years was a big difference until the age of thirty-five, and Julie was *not* thirty-five. Not even close.

Then I did laugh.

"For real? You want the old lady to teach you?"

She nodded.

"How the hell am I supposed to figure this out if you can't?" she asked.

She had a point there. If I, the tech goddess, couldn't figure out how to use a phone app, we were all fucked.

"Fair enough," I agreed. "I'll teach you."

We chatted about the fact that I'd be working from home and that she could, too, if she wanted. It wasn't like Julie didn't have a receptionist as capable as Barb. Julie clearly had more control issues than I did. Then again, she'd been the reason I'd let mine go. With her, I was comfortable enough to let go. I could understand if Julie hadn't gotten there yet.

We talked some more about Cody and Brian, and about things going on in the office Julie was harboring doubts about. I reassured her that there was nothing to worry about on any of those fronts. She knew it, too, just needed to hear it from a voice other than her own. I knew about that all too well.

I wouldn't take back one thing I did

One word I said.

Where the fuck did that come from? I thought I was over killing Dario. Was I somehow not? I nodded in spite of myself. I knew damn well that was how trauma worked. I could be fine for a long time, then, out of nowhere, I'd be throat punched with it. Back to feeling everything as though it had just happened. *FUCK ME!* The internal screams threatened to rip me apart.

I stood.

"I've gotta go. Love you. Call you later," I said, practically running from the office and into my Jeep.

I slammed my forehead against the steering wheel and turned the music up.

Thirteen

I TRULY THOUGHT I was at the point of unbreakable by now. I'd endured Dario's abuse while we were together. Even when we weren't together; that guy had NOTHING over me. Was I deluding myself? Or was I simply not far enough in my healing journey?

On my way home, I couldn't help but be annoyed with myself. I knew that getting over this one would be a challenge. I wanted to call Ben, but what would I say? *Oh, hey, Ben. I killed my narcissistically abusive ex and now I feel stuck in the trauma bond.* Yeah, that would go over like a prostitute walking into a high-class church. Maybe I could just see him for breaking the trauma bond and subsequent healing I knew I needed. I huffed and called.

"Hey, Brit!" He greeted me cheerfully. "I was wondering when I'd hear from you again."

"Been busy," I replied tersely, "When can you fit me in?"

We agreed I'd go in once this week and once a week for the next eight weeks, then reassess. This was going to suck hard, but I felt like I had no choice. I didn't like feeling this way, and no one I chose to be around deserved my lashing out or emotional distance.

When I got home, Stu was sitting on the couch watching something. I was paying little attention when I leaned over to kiss his forehead before walking into the kitchen.

"You okay?" he asked.

How does he always know? Am I that easy to read?

"No," I mumbled, opening a fresh bottle of moscato. "I see Ben later this week and go back weekly for the next eight weeks."

Stu was on me so fast as I spun to grab a glass from the cabinet.

"What's going on?" He wrapped his arms around me in a ginger yet loving embrace. I could feel the empathy and love radiating from him.

"It looks like I'm stuck in a weird cycle of shit leftover from probably not fully processing the breakup with Dario." I chugged my wine and refilled. "The actual breakup years ago."

Stu nodded, accepting that explanation.

"I just... I feel so unlike *me*, if that makes sense. I've been having random nightmares, panic attacks, and reminders popping up seemingly out of nowhere. I'm not okay, and I hate it."

I plopped down onto the floor, not even caring that it hurt my ass bones, and started to cry. Stu sat down next to me and held me, silent. He knew now wasn't a time to talk. Now was a time to let me feel it.

And I felt it. I wondered if these feelings of random sadness would ever go away, or at least lessen. And I felt the sadness profoundly. Scenes ran through my mind of "the good times" that weren't really good times; they were the highest of highs brought on by that—what was it called? —risk-reward cycle.

I'd spent some time listening to a doctor who specialized in narcissistic abuse on YouTube, and she was amazing. It turned out I wasn't the only person who'd experienced these things, and now I had names for them. She even said true healing couldn't begin because we couldn't process what we couldn't name. I felt that in my bones. It was the worst feeling, too.

By the time I was able to breathe normally, my eyes and face hurt. Stu stood and pulled the bottle of wine down from the counter, then handed it to me. I snickered in spite of myself. *Unhealthy coping mechanisms for the win.*

"Weren't we just talking about *not* being alcoholics?" I half joked.

Stu chuckled.

"You're fine, babe," he said.

I continued to drink, not sipping but not chugging, while we sat there. I zoned out on the fridge, and before I lost all sense of vision and space, I felt Stu's eyes on me. He was concerned, and I wouldn't let him in any deeper. After all he'd told me, and I couldn't say any more? What the fuck kind of person was I?

I wondered this so much that it broke me from my trance.

"I'm just not ready to talk about all of it yet."

It came out in a whisper.

Stu replied, but I couldn't hear him over the static in my head. Then I shot upright to my feet like a firework on July the Fourth.

"Grab your shoes. We're going to karaoke," I said before darting from the kitchen to freshen up my face. I heard Stu belt out a laugh on my way up the stairs.

While I was making myself look presentable, Stu had called for a Lyft to take us to the bar at Nebraska and Florida Avenues. As my foot hit the bottom stair, Stu opened the front door. My face showed the confusion my brain was feeling at that moment.

"The car's here," he said, motioning out the open door.

I nodded, smiling, and stepped out into the cool-ish night air.

"Uh, are we still in Florida, Aunt Em?" I asked with a giggle. It was July, and July was *never* even close to nice.

"Uncle Henry," Stu corrected, "And yes. The forecast for the next few days is a nice one."

I shivered a little and kept walking to the end of the driveway, where the car waited for us to get in. When we did, our driver greeted us and backed out. As usual with these types of rides, our driver was awesome. I started to devise a way to gather the information of the truly great ones, and maybe start another business.

The cogs in my head turned, wondering how I could make this a viable business plan. I'd also want to go public with stocks at some point, so that would be something new to research. I shrugged to myself, hoping Stu didn't notice, as we pulled up to the bar. The thoughts only lasted until Stu let me know we'd arrived.

Once inside, I didn't think about it again. I walked over to an empty table and sat in the armchair. Stu trailed behind, and when he walked up to me, the first thing he did was chuckle.

"No hesitation," he remarked.

I grinned.

"Drinks are on you," I replied with a wink.

Stu chuckled again and disappeared. He returned holding a glass of wine in one hand, a pint of beer in the other.

"For my lush," he said, handing me the wine.

I rolled my eyes, smiling.

"Good to know I'm not an alcoholic. But a bottle would have been the better way to go." As I sipped, I glanced at him from the corner of my eye, eyebrow raised.

Stu just smiled and shook his head.

"I only have so many hands."

And the things you can do with them… The words almost came out of my mouth, but I figured those were best said behind closed doors.

Fourteen

SOMEHOW, NEITHER ONE OF us had a hangover the next day. Of course, Stu had to work at some ridiculous time—7 a.m. or something. I, on the other hand, didn't actually start working until nine. So, when I rolled lazily out of bed at eight, I didn't have to rush. Not anymore.

I strolled to the bathroom to get ready, the scent of freshly brewing coffee wafting up the stairs. *The wonders of automatic coffee makers.*

Downstairs, I sat at the kitchen table and booted up my laptop. While it did its thing, I poured coffee over three ice cubes, then stirred. If I didn't stir, the water would sit on top and make it gross. The temperature was far too hot without the cubes, and I really wasn't in a mood to burn my mouth.

I checked my email and saw that the potential client Julie had created the proposal for had accepted it, and I did a little dance in my chair. I hoped she'd seen it by now too and was doing the same thing. Maybe it would even assuage her doubt in her abilities. Doubtful it would take only one, but baby steps.

I distracted myself with work until it was time to head out to Ben's office. When I saw the time, my shoulders slumped, and I sighed. I composed myself and stood, putting my sneakers on and grabbing my things. I even found an empty notebook, so I took it with me hoping that some things Ben could offer would prove useful in some way.

I tried to perk myself up with music on the drive there, but it didn't help. By the time I parked in the lot, I was still dreading seeing him, regretting making the series of appointments at all. But I knew I couldn't continue like this, so I got out of my Jeep and walked in.

Ben seemed to materialize from his office into the waiting room. I hadn't even had a chance to sit down.

"Hey, Brit, come on back," he said, swinging his arm like an old person would, motioning for me to go into his private office.

I strode in and sat on the couch. The stereotype to end all stereotypes. At that moment, I wished he had plastic chairs. Anything to avoid this feeling more cliché than it already did. But I wasn't a magician, and the couch still existed. I flopped down with a whooshing sound.

Ben sat in his chair across from me, notepad on his lap, pen in his hand. So very cliché.

"So?" he asked.

That was the opening I was waiting for. I launched into the unresolved feelings I had about my relationship—if that's what you would call it—with Dario. The verbal, emotional, and mental abuse, the highs, the underground lows—all of it. I even told him about the doctor I'd been listening to online.

He nodded his head in agreement, surprising me.

"What was her name again?"

I told him, and he scribbled it down.

"I'd heard about these things, been told about them by other patients. Now I need to learn how to treat them."

Well then. That was a surprise. All this time he'd come off almost as a know-it-all, and here he sat, admitting to me that he had things he needed to learn because he simply didn't know. Ben would make some lucky person truly happy one day. If he ever dated.

He and I had known each other long enough for me to know that dating was a rare thing for him. It wasn't that he wasn't interested, but also, he wasn't interested. I understood that.

Stu had fallen into my lap. I'd shot a fellow cop, and he was the first to arrive. Now we were engaged. But at the time, I had no interest, but also had interest. This didn't make sense to a lot of people close to me, probably because they'd never felt that contradiction inside.

I started back up again and Ben the Studious took his notes.

By the time my hour was up, I felt lighter for having gotten it all out to someone. No one—NO ONE—knew these things. The things Dario said and did to me, my feelings about it all—nothing. Not even Stu.

"Have you told Stu any of this?" Ben asked, pulling me from my contemplation.

I stared at him blankly.

"You probably should. I mean, if you're going to spend the rest of your life with him, he deserves to know."

"Deserves?" I echoed. "*He* deserves? What about me?"

Ben looked down at his notepad, and I didn't know if it was in thought or shame.

"Yes, deserves. Remember, any relation isn't just about you. We can't truly understand those around us without having some kind of idea of the things that make them *them*."

That made too much sense. Stu had opened up to me about his past. I'd told him all of jack and shit about mine. Fair was fair, and I hadn't been.

I nodded, acknowledging Ben's point.

"He did tell me about his childhood," I said, "And he knows nothing of mine or Dario. But where do I start?"

Ben smiled.

"Anywhere you want to. You've kept him in the dark for so long, it doesn't matter. From the beginning would make sense so he doesn't get confused by you jumping from time to time," he suggested.

Again, I nodded.

Ben looked at the clock on the table next to me. I knew what that meant and stood, brushing my thighs off nervously.

"Next week?" I asked.

"Yes. And Brit? If you need to talk more..."

"I know. Thank you," I said, smiling half-heartedly.

He didn't bother making me pay right then. Instead, he'd bill me. That was the arrangement we had. But at this moment, I changed that.

"Hey, Ben? Just start charging my card every time we meet or I call and it's billable."

He nodded. And I walked out into the Florida sun.

It felt like it was cleansing me. Could it? Was it? Or was it the therapy session I'd just had?

Once I was in my Jeep, I texted Stu:

> Can't wait to see you.

I started the engine and called Joe.

"Hi, Brit," he greeted. "To what do I owe the pleasure?"

"Um, we haven't talked much lately, and I wanted to see if you're free for lunch."

It was only 11 a.m., so we had a small amount of time to decide.

"Meet you at Capital Grille at 1," he said.

I grinned.

"Of course."

I went home and changed; leggings and a T-shirt were hardly appropriate. If Joe had said to meet him at his house or somewhere less fancy, I'd have been okay. Given mine and Joe's reputations as they were, leggings wouldn't entirely be…presentable. Especially when Joe would be dressed in his office attire. I worked from home now, so office attire wasn't a way of life anymore.

I made it to International Mall just in time to catch Joe on his way in.

Joe was standing on the sidewalk a few feet from the entrance to Capital Grille, checking his phone. I hopped down from my Jeep and yelled, "Joe," as I waved.

He turned and saw me, waving back.

I wrapped my arm in his, and we walked in.

Fifteen

We both had to work after lunch, but that didn't stop me from ordering wine. *Just a lush. Right. Oh, Stu.*

A lush was likely something I was far away from, but I let myself believe it today. Two glasses of wine over lunch did not an alcoholic make. Right?

Just then, the song "Won't Back Down" by Fuel started in my head…

I tried not to sigh aloud, but it came out.

"You okay?" Joe asked.

"Uh, yeah. Yeah, I'm okay," I lied.

I couldn't tell him. I wouldn't. That was the last thing I'd ever tell him. Hell, even on my death bed, I couldn't see me telling him who—what—I was. Joe was one of the two people on this planet who could never know because it would destroy them. The other was my father.

Besides, it's none of his business.

I was right, of course, but still. I couldn't help but feel like shit.

"So," Joe started as the server brought our drinks, "how have you been? I know you well enough to know you're not yourself lately. You haven't called, texted, stopped by the office…"

I sipped my wine, figuring out how I was going to respond, and set the glass down.

"I haven't," I admitted. "And to be completely honest, Joe, it's none of your business. I love you as much as I love my own father, but it's none of his business either. I have some things I need to work through, and I'm seeing a therapist for them."

I had been absentmindedly swirling my glass while I spoke, and when I realized I'd been doing this, I smirked before taking more than a single sip.

The server came back just then to take our order. We placed those, and as soon as the server left, I felt like I was being attacked, even though Joe meant no such thing.

"Brit," he began, "I see something inside you has…broken."

I nodded in agreement.

"Are you okay? What can I do to help you feel better?" He asked.

I shook my head.

"There's really nothing," I said. "It's just something I've got to fix on my own. Well, with the help of my therapist."

Joe took that and accepted it. I may not have been familiar with his demons, but it felt like he was with mine. How could he not have been, being a plastic surgeon? He saw demons every second of every day. But demons like mine? Ha.

Regardless, I took it at face value. I knew better than to question Joe on his judgment. It had been rather impeccable, including him being my "surrogate."

I was unusually quiet during lunch, letting Joe fill me in on the goings on in his life. Besides, there wasn't much in mine to tell him about.

"What about you?" I heard him ask.

"Not much really. Julie finally wrote her first contract proposal and landed the client," I said beaming.

Joe grinned.

"It's about time! Please tell her I said congratulations."

"I will," I said. "Seriously, I'm so proud of her. You should have seen how nervous she was when she wrote it." I sniggered. "She made me read it right then and there. I told her it was perfect, but she didn't believe me until they signed it."

Joe smiled. "That's how I've always felt about you."

My face turned bright red, and I felt the heat.

"Thanks," I muttered with an impatient shake of my head. I'd always been bad at taking compliments from people I respected. Taking them from strangers was easier—I could brush them off like I believed them. With those I respected, however, I couldn't get away with fake belief, and I knew it. Those people respected me equally and were much more observant of my behaviors and mannerisms than strangers.

"Have you set a date yet?" Joe asked.

His question caused me to choke on my wine.

"No," I managed. It sounded foreign to me, like it wasn't my voice. But it was the truth.

I hadn't thought anything about making wedding plans since Stu's proposal. I'd been so wrapped up in the trauma of killing one of my abusers that I'd thought about little else.

"When we set one, you'll be the first to know," I told him.

He nodded. "Good. I'd like to pay for it. It's the least I can do."

I dropped my fork on the floor as I unraveled my napkin somewhat on purpose.

"No," I told him. "I couldn't let you do that."

"You can and you will. You're the daughter I should've had. We won't discuss that the biological one doesn't speak to me because of her mother. You're going to swallow your pride and let me do this for you." He'd said it so matter-of-factly, so sternly, that even if I had wanted to try to fight him, I couldn't. A father's final say.

"Thank you," was all I could say that he'd accept.

Joe just nodded.

"You're welcome," he said after a few moments of silence. I hoped he'd realized how much it took for me to swallow my pride and say that.

The conversation continued as though that weird break never existed. I supposed that meant Joe realized what it took for me to concede. The food came, and we kept talking while we ate.

Before parting, we hugged, me thanking him again for deciding to pay for my wedding to Stu as the valet pulled his Mercedes around. While I waited for my Jeep, I mulled over how I would broach this conversation with Stu. Then my car pulled up. I tipped the guy and hopped into the driver's seat. As I pulled away, I nodded in acknowledgment of what I'd say.

As soon as I'd turned onto West Boy Scout, my phone rang. It was Stu.

"Hey babe," I greeted.

"Will you be home soon? I miss you and just want you in my arms."

That was unusual. He was rarely the one who said these things; it was usually me.

"Everything okay?" I asked.

"Yeah, I just want to hold you," he said, sounding far away.

Something happened this morning while he was working. That much was clear. What it was, I wouldn't find out until I got home.

Sixteen

AS I WALKED THROUGH the front door, Stu accosted me with hugs. Something had definitely happened while he was working.

"Shouldn't you still be at work?" I asked.

"They sent me home," he whispered in my ear.

Okay, something is wrong here. Really wrong.

I pushed him back to arm's length.

"What happened?"

He shook his head.

"The only thing that could fuck me up like this."

A kid. A kid was killed, and he was somehow the first on scene. It was a gut feeling but I needed to be sure.

"A kid?"

He nodded.

"Fuck." It was all I could say before pulling him close.

Neither one of us knew the kid but the fact that an innocent had been killed fucked with both of us.

I carefully maneuvered us to the couch so he could completely fall apart without knocking me over. Then I fell apart, too. Not in the same way he had, but in a sadness and solidarity. And also in a depression that an innocent life had been taken. I didn't know the circumstances, and I didn't care. A child had been killed, and somehow Stu felt responsible because he was the one on watch then; it was his shift. I did too. And I wasn't a cop.

Days like this made me glad I wasn't. I'd have done things that Stu was capable of not. Me? I'd have blacked out and lost my mind on someone.

"Talk to me," I whispered in a husky tone.

"The poor girl... Her mom cheated on her dad, and... She did nothing... Dad went to shoot mom, and..."

She got caught in the crossfire.

"How old was she?"

"Five." His voice broke, and he sobbed into my chest.

My eyes welled up, and I lost it with him. He'd only recently let me into his past. He was five when his mother had started abusing him. For all I knew, he was mourning the loss of his innocence, too. But this girl was caught in the middle. He'd never been that fortunate. Maybe he was mourning not just the loss of innocence but the fact that he wasn't that lucky.

I held him as tight as I could, feeling his sadness. *Am I broken? I've never felt anyone else's pain so acutely before.* It was all I could do, all I knew to do. We sobbed together for a long time until everything went black.

I opened my eyes to the screensaver on the TV showing 10 p.m. As I shifted to ease the pain in my left knee, Stu woke up.

"I'm sorry, babe. Go back to sleep," I cooed.

I slid from the couch and walked into the kitchen. I needed something to make the nightmare quiet down. Wine would do the trick.

"Grab me one," I heard from the living room, and I did as I was asked. It was the least I could do. I knew damn well I couldn't do much else for this specific trauma. Then I started to wonder what he'd say during the psych evaluation that was sure to follow. The majority of me didn't want to know.

I grabbed a couple of beers for Stu and the bottle of wine for me. I didn't know how much longer we'd be down here with our unhealthy coping mechanisms, but I wanted us to be prepared.

I handed Stu a beer as I sat back down on the couch. He tapped the rim of it against my glass that I'd just finished pouring and took a big swig. I took a mouthful of mine as Stu pressed Play on I-had-no-idea-what.

As I sat back to relax, Stu wrapped an arm around my shoulders and set his free hand on my thigh. While this was totally normal for him, it also wasn't. He was hurting. And there was nothing I could do to ease that pain.

That was the thing—the problem—with dating and being engaged to a cop. They saw some truly heinous shit, and there was nothing you could do about it. There was no verbiage for how much that sucked. You felt like you failed them somehow because of your inability to actually help. You knew this fact going into a relationship with them, but that didn't make it suck any less.

I rested my hand on top of his to let him know I was there. Not that I thought he didn't already know that, but I wanted him to feel it. If anyone on this planet understood anything about pain. I knew that I had my own feelings about this situation and for Stu and how he felt. I knew that I was also all too capable of tuning those feelings out.

Maybe, just maybe, I'd take it all out on my newest victim. It wasn't like she didn't already deserve to die, the cunt. Katie would get what was coming to her. Every last bit of it. For now, though, I needed to compartmentalize all the things I was feeling.

I cleared my throat.

"Joe wants to pay for our wedding. He wouldn't take no for an answer, so I agreed. Reluctantly," I said in the span of a single breath.

"Okay," Stu replied.

I couldn't believe what I was hearing.

"Say that again?"

"Okay," he stated. "It's not like we wouldn't be paying on it for the next ten years of our lives if we paid for it on our own."

He had a point.

"As long as one of us is cool with it," I muttered.

Stu turned to me.

"Look, Joe can give you everything you want for our wedding. We could, too, but as I said before, we'd be paying for it—plus interest—for at least ten years afterward. Neither one of us has that kind of cash."

I wanted to say something spiteful in retort, but I had nothing. I was spectacularly full of nothing except a head full of fuzz and sleep.

And frustration. For my inability to tell Stu anytime soon about the things that made me *me*, that I was sorry I couldn't take his pain away. For so many things.

I wanted nothing more than to be able to tell him everything after my session with Ben. But how could I now without looking like a narcissist?

Seventeen

THE DAY HAD COME for Stu's psych evaluation, and I was pretty sure I was more nervous than he was about it.

"And what do you think would go so wrong?" he asked.

I shook my head and lifted my hands up, helpless.

"I don't know, but I don't see how you can *not* look like a psychopath," I responded.

"Ye of little faith," he said with a grin and a wink.

I chuckled in spite of myself. He was right. And he knew it. He was completely able to make it look like he wasn't the detached person he actually was because he wasn't entirely detached.

I, however, was now the one making herself look totally insane. I sighed and continued getting dressed for the day.

Stu was finished before me and brought me up a cup of coffee as I was putting my makeup on.

"I don't even know why I'm doing this," I said to him.

"Doing what?" he asked as he set the mug down on the countertop.

"Putting makeup on. I don't see anyone, and they don't see me. Not even over video."

"You take pride in your appearance," he replied, as though it was a fact so simple even a child could grasp it.

I rolled my eyes in disbelief. But again, he was right. I did take pride in my appearance. Most of the time. It didn't matter in the times I felt like true shit, like right after I killed Dario. It killed me inside that I was so transparent to Stu.

He kissed me on the cheek.

"Well, I have to go if I want to make it to the shrink on time." He buttoned up his uniform shirt as he spoke.

I stopped doing my makeup and checked him out like we just met.

"You're hot," I commented.

He smiled.

"Thanks."

When he'd finished buttoning up, he kissed me again and left.

I waited about thirty seconds before calling down the stairs after him.

"You've got this and will be back on patrol before you know it!"

I didn't know a thing about how long an administrative leave like this lasted. Was it until the shrink cleared him? Was it longer? The only person I could ask had just left, and I wasn't exactly comfortable asking him anyway.

When I walked into the kitchen to open my laptop, I noticed the sliding door was open. *Did Stu open that and forget to tell me?*

I walked out onto the patio and felt what could have been the worst humidity I'd ever felt.

"Gross," I said to no one and wiped the film off my arms that had formed as quickly as I'd been outside.

Back inside, I felt like I needed another shower but also knew I could take one over my lunch break or whenever I wanted. Right now wasn't that time. I only just finished my makeup and didn't want to waste it—I looked damn good.

I opened my laptop at the kitchen table and checked my email first. At the top was one from Katie.

"What now?" I groaned.

The more I read the too-long email, the more the idea in my head grew. This cunt had to go. I was able to clearly imagine how she treated those around her just from reading what she'd written to me. She was Dario but worse and female. She was almost my mother. The decision was now cemented. Only one question remained: How much should she suffer?

I picked up the phone and called the publishing company I'd originally wanted to place Katie with.

"How may I direct your call?" the woman on the other end asked.

"Erika Logan, please," I replied.

"Please hold."

I got her voice mail, so I left a message.

Erika and I had met a little while back, and I knew that if there was one person who would put Katie in her place as an employer, it was Erika. She was no nonsense and valued quality over quantity. That was all I needed to know about her.

It didn't matter that the voice in my head told me she'd eventually have to die, too. It didn't matter that I thought her contracts were a bit less than ideal for the authors she signed. Though I did think a 60/40 split to the publisher was more than fair since they covered everything up front. My problem was that that percentage never changed. But I also knew indies got fucked hard unless they handled everything themselves.

Personal feelings aside, I knew if I could get Katie placed there, she wouldn't be missed if she disappeared. Not that the attorneys would miss her, either. Besides, I had a feeling about Erika I couldn't shake. I needed to get to know her one way or another.

Erika didn't call me back in time to start Katie; she'd already started at the law office as a researcher so no one would really *have* to interact with her, which was better for me for multiple reasons. The first—and most important—being that I wouldn't risk a contract being severed.

She did call me back later that week and agreed to meet me for lunch under the pretenses of getting to know her and her company better. It was a good time. She wasn't at all what I expected.

I truly believed she was as ruthless as I was. She wasn't. She was smart, really smart, but kind in her business dealings. That struck me as sort of out of place. Was she like that to put on a show for me, or was that who she truly was?

It didn't matter right now. I needed to dispatch of Katie the Cunt first. Erika was on my back burner.

Eighteen

It was midweek when I called Katie into the office. I'd come in just for this meeting with her, and Barb knew it. She'd even asked if Katie was in trouble since I didn't usually do things like this.

"Nope," I replied almost too happily.

"Soooo…"

"I want to get to know her better is all."

Barb had nodded her acknowledgment, and that was that. She left it alone.

When Katie knocked on the doorframe, I looked up and smiled, waving her in.

"Close the door." She did as she was told, asking me, "Am I in some kind of trouble?"

"Not at all," I said. "I just want to get to know you, your preferences, and skills, better. I get the feeling you being in my employment is a fluke. I want to make sure I'm able to make you happy while you're here."

I used the word *happy* on purpose, knowing she was incapable of such feelings. That was the biggest difference between her and me. And she knew it, too.

Katie sat down, eying me cautiously."I'm really not in any kind of trouble?" she half asked half stated.

I shook my head.

"Nope. So, you're a teacher, right?"

She nodded.

"Okay, so that makes you a fit for a lot of different positions," I started.

She held up a hand. *So fucking rude. And we know what the good doctor said about the rude. Not this nasty cunt, though.* I shuddered.

We talked work a little bit longer before I got more personal.

"So, what do you like to do in your free time? Do you drink wine?"

She cocked her head to the side, trying to gauge me and my intentions. I was intentionally flat. I knew all too well how to behave around narcissists. After all, I'd been raised by the worst kind.

"I do like wine," she ceded, "though I prefer gin. And in my free time I like to go for walks."

Uh-huh. Walks. Right.

"How about you meet me for drinks one night?"

"Miss Cage, I don't know that's appropriate."

"Hush. It's fine. No conflicts. It would be a conflict if I was one of the attorneys you were doing research for. Me? Ha," I replied, flourishing my hand at the end for dramatic flair.

She hesitated for a moment before replying.

"Okay. I think I could do that. Did you have a day in mind?"

"As a matter of fact"—I flipped through my desk calendar— "how does next week look for you? I'm wide open."

Katie pulled a planner from her bag—my kind of woman, carrying a paper planner with her everywhere she went. But also the teacher in her.

"Next week looks good for me, but can I get back to you about the day? The research has been exhausting," she said.

"Sure. Let me know."

She stood and turned on her heel to leave.

"Katie," I said, standing.

She spun to face me.

"You'll be a teacher again." I smiled.

"I know," she replied.

This bitch...

I waited about ten minutes after she left before I grabbed my bag and left myself out. Barb stopped me on my way out.

"She's...a challenge, no?"

I laughed sardonically.

"Yes. Yes, she is," I agreed. "She's someone I'd never want in my personal life, that's for sure."

Barb shuddered visibly.

"Me either. She's so bitchy." She cleared her throat. "Excuse me for that."

I shook my head.

"Don't worry about it. You're not wrong. And Barb? You can always be honest with me," I said before adjusting my bag on my shoulder and walking out.

At home, I gave Minion fresh water and opened my laptop to get back to work when my cell rang. It was Julie.

"Hey!"

"Hi, Brit! So, I was wondering if it was okay for me to write more proposals. I met with a few potential clients today, and—"

"Yes," I cut in. "Always yes. You're a natural."

She chuckled uncomfortably.

"Thanks.""So, tell me about these clients?" I asked.

Julie rambled excitedly about the four different clients she'd met with this week, three today alone. They were all established companies in the area and wanted to switch the temp agency they used for one more consistently high-rated.

A magnificent smile spread on my face. Not only was Julie meeting with these clients, and they *wanted* to work with us, but I'd somehow lost track of my company's satisfaction ratings on places like Glassdoor. I scribbled a note to set a recurring reminder on Barb's calendar to check the ratings twice a week. It was something we could—and would—use to our benefit.

"Damn, Jules! You're killin' it!"

"Thanks," she replied. "I'm still getting used to all the compliments on how we run the company."

"Yeah, that'll take a bit. But the ones from me better not take much longer," I half joked. "In all seriousness, I'm trying to help you build your self-confidence. The more you hear the good, the easier it gets to accept it and build off it. I speak from experience."

She sighed.

"I know. And I'm trying, I really am. I just…Well, I don't actually know why it hasn't gotten easier yet," she admitted.

"Because you won't let it," I stated.

She was silent for a while.

"You know…"

I nodded even though she couldn't see me.

"Yep. I know." I grinned, hoping she could hear it on the other end.

"Subject change. When are you and Stu coming over for dinner? Brian misses you and wants to see you."

"Uh… I honestly have no idea. Stu had an incident at work, and I don't know if he's ready to be around kids again yet. I'll ask him."

I didn't realize how poorly I'd worded the situation until all of the words fell out of my mouth.

"Is he okay?" Julie asked.

Whew! She doesn't think it's as bad as I accidentally made it sound.

"He will be. I'll text you after I talk to him. Did you have any days in mind?"

"Nope. Just wanted to ask."

"Okay, cool. I'll get back to you. Worst case is I come scoop up Brian and hang with him just the two of us. It's been a while since we did that."

"Brit, he'd love that!"

I heard the door chime go off in the background.

"Shit, I have to go. Talk to you later!"

I couldn't even say bye back before she hung up. I hoped it was more potential clients.

Nineteen

WHEN STU GOT HOME, I was in the kitchen dancing to loud music and making dinner. He walked in and wrapped his arms around my waist, nuzzling my neck.

I set the spatula down and spun, wrapping my arms around his neck, and kissed him.

"How did it go?" I asked.

"Pretty good. I'm on desk duty for another two weeks, though," he replied, grumbling the last part.

I didn't know how to respond to that.

"Is that good?""Could be better, but at least they're not keeping me out," he replied from the refrigerator.

He pulled out the iced tea and poured a glass. "Want some?"

I nodded, and he poured another. It would be nice to have something nonalcoholic for a change.

Stu sat at the table alternating playing with his glass and sipping from it. I eyed him carefully until he looked up at me.

"What's going through your head?"

I shook my head.

"Nothing," I lied.

"Bullshit. Talk to me."

I wanted to. Fuck, I wanted to. But there was no way I could and feel okay with it.

"It's nothing. Really." Even *I* didn't believe me.

Stu came over to me as I spun around to "check" on dinner. He placed his hands on my shoulders and gently turned me to face him.

"Try again," he said, his face showing nothing but concern. "If you're not okay, then neither am I."

The spite I suddenly felt for myself after that slap in the face was tangible.

I let out a sigh, my shoulders dropping from my ears.

"Fine. But I need you to remember it wasn't me forcing it out on you."

Stu nodded, a half smile on his face.

I proceeded to tell him of my childhood and the vilest person on the planet—vilest to me, anyway. I elaborated on so many things he only knew glimpses of. My mother; my best friend, Cassie; all of it. I even went into more detail about Sweet.

"Heh, I already knew that," he commented when I talked about Sweet.

"You *knew* I was seeing him to cover my tracks?" I was incredulous.

He nodded.

"Come on, he's nowhere near as good looking as me." He laughed.

I giggled, and it felt good. I felt so much better telling him every last detail of what made me *me*.

"I feel so much better now that you know all of it," I said. "Is this how you felt?"

"High? Yeah." He nodded.

"Shit." It was all I could say.

My mouth was dry. I picked up my tea and sipped it, swishing it around my mouth before swallowing.

Stu walked back over to the table to take a sip of his.

I finished making dinner and set it all out on the table, with light banter between us. When I finally sat down, Stu smiled at me, the twinkle in his eye returning.

"Now that we are both feeling better, I have something to ask you," I said.

Way to go, Brit. You lay all your weight on him and then one-two punch him with the Brian question.

"Julie asked me when we'd be able to make it over there for dinner. She said Brian misses me. I'm okay with just him-and-me time. And next week Katie and I are meeting for drinks."

Stu didn't move except to look up at me from his plate, one eyebrow cocked.

"You're going for drinks with who now? I thought you hated her."

"I do, and she's next on my list. Which is why we're meeting for drinks. I need to get to know her a little bit before beginning."

He picked his head up, fully facing me.

"I get it. As for Brian, I'm okay with going there for dinner. I can be around kids I know. I think."

He picked up his fork and dropped his attention back down to his plate.

"Babe, if you're not sure, let's wait," I suggested.

"No, no, it's fine. Let's try it. If something in my head gets weird, I'll just leave and come back for you," he said.

I shrugged. There was nothing else I could do. He wasn't having me tell Julie no, but he wasn't outright saying yes.

"Sure," I mumbled as I poked at my salad with my fork.

Stu's eyes pleaded with mine, and I stared right back.

"Fine," I huffed. "I'll let her know after dinner." Stu grinned.

"You're such a pushover," he chided.

I smiled. I hadn't realized how important it was for him to test himself. But this was Julie. And Cody and Brian. Julie wouldn't cheat, and neither would Cody. There was nothing for Brian to get caught in the middle of. *Am I looking at this from the wrong perspective?*

"Am I looking at this from the wrong perspective?" I asked him.

Stu cleared his throat after nearly choking on his iced tea.

"Come again?"

"Am I looking at this from the wrong perspective?" I repeated. "Julie would never cheat. Cody would never cheat. So, Brian would never be caught in the middle—" I stopped short, unsure how to save this.

Stu chuckled.

"It's not about who's involved. It's about the fact that an innocent child died at the hands of her father. Someone she told she loves on a daily basis—" He choked up, fought it back, and gathered himself.

I dropped my fork onto my plate, causing more of a scene in my own home than coming off as understanding. I placed a hand gingerly on his.

"I'm sorry. I didn't mean to come off as insensitive. And your reaction settles it. I'll hang out with Brian, just us."

"You will not. I mean, you can, but I want to go over there for dinner," Stu said forcefully enough that I pushed my chair back from the table, unsure if I should hug him or go for one of my many guns. Which were all upstairs. *Dammit!*

I sat there, not frozen. But unmoving. We locked eyes again, and I didn't turn away. These days were long gone; a million years ago. Stu didn't back down either. We just glared at each other, neither of us harboring any ill will toward the other. I honestly believed we were locked in a weird standoff of misunderstanding. Like hostage takers and cops.

Stu broke first when he slumped.

"I didn't mean that the way it came out." He stood from his chair and walked around the table to mine. "And I didn't mean to scare you. I'm just... Okay, maybe you're right. Maybe I'm being stupid or stubborn, but I want to try it. Please?"

I held my hands up.

"If that's what you want."

Stu nodded.

"Okay. I'll let Julie know."

I began cleaning up my seat at the table, not hungry enough to actually sit down to try to eat more than the three pieces of chicken and handful of lettuce I'd already eaten.

Stu helped me finish clearing the table and then loaded the dishwasher.

When we were done, I started the tub in my bathroom.

I loaded it up with aromatic scents like lavender and eucalyptus. I needed calming, and I wasn't sure why. I wished I had unscented bubbles, but all I had were rose scented, and that would make for a knock-out combination. Like the one in the Bog of Eternal Stench.

Stu came in while I was lying there in the water, eyes closed, trying to come to grips with everything that had happened in the past week. He sat on the edge of the tub.

"You okay?"

My eyes popped open. I didn't know he had come in at all.

"Mm-hmm." I nodded as I made the sound.

This felt backward. Like I should be the one asking him.

"You're not," he stated.

I heaved a sigh. "Why do you have to know me so well?" I sat up, wrapping my arms around my bent knees. "I'm confused and stressed out about taking you to a dinner neither one of us knows if you're ready for."

Stu smiled.

"I'm not. How else will we know what I'm ready for?"

He had a point, and I didn't want to agree, but…

I nodded. "I understand that."

"So you're okay now?"

I chortled.

"No, but I will be." I sat up to kiss him, lay back down, and closed my eyes.

Twenty

A FEW DAYS LATER, Katie called to let me know when she'd be able to have drinks. We settled on Tuesday since I had dinner plans with Julie on Thursday and those were Katie's free days.

I snickered as I hung up the phone; I would have this bitch on the other end of my knife soon enough. Which reminded me of something I didn't know how or why I'd forgotten: the stalking. *How does a killer forget that she needs to stalk her prey? Stop it. You've been through a lot these past few months.* At least I wasn't yelling at myself out loud?

I did need to start the game, but not today. Hell, maybe not even this week. I got the feeling that not only was she a narcissist, but she was the kind that harbored no remorse or paranoia. That could go either way, and it wasn't something I was willing to risk. I'd start following her in a couple weeks. Besides, I had to work out this weird shit in my head and heart with Ben, and it was time to head to his office anyway.

When I walked in, he was sitting on a chair in the waiting area, reading a magazine. I cocked my head to the side.

"Catching up on the latest celebrity lies?" I asked. Ben snickered.

"Hardly. I needed something to keep me busy, and the internet wasn't enough to take me down a rabbit hole. I've been here alone all day with all of my appointments needing to reschedule." He sighed. I got the vibe that he truly felt bad that I was the only one he would help today.

I motioned with my arm to his office.

"Vamos! I've got shit to talk about and I'm not paying you to read that trash," I half joked.

He grinned as he shot up from the chair and led the way back.

I sat on the clichéd couch while Ben grabbed and properly positioned his notepad. When he looked up at me, I began.

I made a conscious effort to only speak about my mother—though she never deserved the title—and Dario for the next forty-five minutes. The remaining fifteen, Ben gave me practical ways to combat the thoughts and feelings.

He'd finally started teaching me how to not only cope but deal with these issues like the adult I was. And heal.

By the time I got back home, I was feeling much better. Well, minus the fact that I had to get back to work. *That's* how good I was feeling. If I didn't have to sit back down in front of my laptop, I'd have been on my way to the beach.

And there's your age showing, Brit.

I cackled. I always did this—felt my age then thought about being my age. I shrugged. Life wasn't all sunshine and sand for me, and I was happy with that. It took a lot of energy to be the entrepreneur control freak I was.

Luckily, it was only an hour or two worth of work I had to finish before I could start dinner. But as soon as I'd started preheating pans, my phone rang a specific ringtone. I grinned as I picked up my cell.

"Hey there, my sexy, strapping man," I cooed.

Stu laughed.

"Hey, babe! I'm on my way home now and knew you'd probably be cooking, but I want to take you out for dinner tonight."

"What's the occasion?"

"Isn't just because a good enough reason?"

It was my turn to laugh.

"It is," I replied with a nod.

"Good. See you in ten."

"Love you," I said.

"Love you, too," Stu responded. Then the line cut off.

I giggled, knowing he wasn't a big fan of always saying that like I was. I didn't care because, as a serial killer, I knew how short life really was. And I truly valued that fact.

Knowing Stu would still need to change, I took my time turning the burners off and putting away the things I'd taken out. By the time I was finished, Stu walked in and raced up the stairs.

I smirked, then jogged up behind him.

He was in the closet changing his pants, and I caught him with one leg in, one leg out.

"That's a hot look on you," I rasped in my best phone sex operator voice.

He stumbled, laughing.

"You almost got me!"

I chuckled and pulled a dress down, holding it against myself in the full-length mirror.

Stu came up behind me and whispered in my ear.

"It doesn't matter what you wear, you're always sexy. Besides, the floor will be the one wearing it the longest."

Then he kissed my neck, and I started to melt before shooing him off.

"Well, I guess I need to wear panties now…"

We both finished changing and headed out to Gen X Tavern. It wasn't a fancy place, but that didn't matter—we weren't dressed fancy. More than casual, but not fancy. Most people were there in khaki pants or shorts, but we didn't care, and neither did they. After all, Gen X cared about nothing; they were the most apathetic generation ever, and deservedly so.

Stu and I were just outside Gen X, but we heavily identified with them, both of us sharing the same sense of apathy having been abused and neglected.

We had a great time with great food and good drinks. Stu even limited how many he had so he could drive home. It made me glad to have a fiancé who was a cop but not the douchey kind who thought he could get away with drunk driving.

It was game on when we walked through the front door. Clothes dropped to the floor, leaving a picturesque trail up to our bedroom, where we showed each other how much we loved each other before falling asleep.

I caught myself waking up an hour later to thoughts of *How great will it be in ten years and we still act this way, all hot for each other*.

My mouth was dry, so I walked into the bathroom, drank the nasty tap water, and crawled back into bed beside Stu. I snuggled up to him and laid my head on his chest before falling into a coma of sleep.

Twenty-One

THE NEXT MORNING, I didn't bother picking out decent clothes. I'd be home all day and needed to look presentable for my date with a cunt. I only used that word when appropriate, and for Katie, it was. So, trading looks for comfort, I pulled on sweats and did my makeup. Clothes would wait until later.

Stu had the day off but had things to do. He also decided to get our grocery shopping done. *Thank fucking God. I hate doing that.* Not that it would keep him out of the house all day, but for a few hours. And when he was home, I knew he would do his best not to disturb my ability to work.

Which he didn't, except when he brought in and put away all the groceries. I offered to help, but he wasn't hearing it.

"You need to focus," he said.

I scoffed.

"Well, I can't really do that with all that bag rustling you're doing," I retorted playfully.

"You could—"

"No," I cut him off, "I'm not going into the other room. I was playing with you. Geez."

Stu grinned at me.

"I know," he replied, then went back to putting the dry goods away.

Around 4:30, I headed upstairs to change before meeting Katie, pausing to kiss the top of Stu's head as he sat on the couch catching up on Sports-Center.

When I came back down, Stu whistled.

"Hey, sexy! You got a date tonight?"

I threw my head back and laughed.

"I hope we're still like this at sixty."

Stu arched a brow then grinned.

"Duh," he responded before pulling me in to kiss me.

I left soon after, promising to be home before ten. Stu had ideas of things he wanted to do before bed. Things you only read about in books like that mommy porn crap that was essentially shitty vampire fan fiction. The thought did things to me, aside from blushing and giggling like a schoolgirl.

Katie and I met at The Pub, my usual place for dinner with the girls, but also in the middle of both of our homes.

We chatted about how the research position was going for her, and she complained abrout it. I doubted her when she'd first said how much she enjoyed it because I knew better.

"I can put you somewhere else," I offered, sipping my drink.

She shook her head.

"It's a nice break from teenagers," she replied, the venom of hatred obvious in her tone.

I shrugged, not about to bend more for her. I didn't normally offer switching posts to anyone unless they truly were struggling. From the feedback I was receiving from the law office, Katie was definitely not struggling. Quite the opposite. *Fucking narcissistic piece of shit.*

About an hour in, Katie had polished off a whole bottle of gin by herself. She opened like a rose blooming, though she didn't smell anywhere near as good.

She had two children and an ex-husband. She'd fucked them all over when she slept with her husband's now former best friend. Her girls hated her, though they played the game. That much I could tell even if she couldn't. She *wanted* to believe they actually wanted to spend time with her. If the walls in her place could talk, I was sure they'd be able to write a self-help book.

By the time we left, I knew her whole life story and then some. More than I'd ever imagined she'd tell me, and to say I was grossed out and thoroughly revolted would be an extreme understatement. But I'd also have a lot to use against her when I told her why she was about to die. I sneered maliciously as I waited for the valet to pull my Jeep around and she'd walked into the lot.

Finally out on Dale Mabry, I talked to myself.

"She's going down, that cunt. She deserves more than just a knife to the heart; she deserves to be tortured like those twatty sisters a few years ago."

Then I heard it. The song that expressed how I always felt pre-kill: "Go to Sleep" by Eminem, DMX, and Obie Trice. I liked how Eminem said he wasn't going to sleep until his nemesis was dead. I felt the same way about Katie the Cunt. I bopped my head and sang the along until it was over. And I was still high from it by the time I backed into my garage.

"Hmm," I wondered aloud.

When I went inside, Stu was still on the couch watching SportsCenter.

"Men," I huffed with a smirk, walking past him to put my shoes by the door.

"What?" he almost whined. "I've missed all of my games this week."

"All? What? Just one?" I retorted, grinning.

"Hush, you," he replied patting the couch next to where he sat. "Tell me all about tonight."

I sat and launched into all the things Katie had told me about her and her life. Stu nodded along with what I was saying until I finished.

"So? What's the verdict?" I snorted.

"Do you even need to ask?"

He turned to face me and grinned.

I kissed him and we turned into teenagers like we had the night before, right there on the couch. Sometimes other pieces of furniture needed their share of bodily fluids, too.

Two days later, I was an almost nervous wreck. Almost because I wasn't in total nervous mode, but all it would take was another three minutes inside my own head. I'd been frantically trying to pick out clothes to wear to Julie's house for dinner when Stu came home.

He let out a "tsk" me when he walked into the closet.

"It doesn't matter what you wear. You're always beautiful," he said. "And stop freaking out. I'll be fine."

I tried to smile like I meant it, but it looked like I was actively trying to swallow my face.

Stu snorted.

"Wow! That was the worst fake I've ever seen. And I've seen a lot of faking," he joked.

My face flushed.

"I know you feel okay, but what if—"

"What if I'm not?" he finished.

I nodded.

"I'm fine," he reiterated.

"Okay, well then, get changed," I said, poking him in the ribs.

He was ready to go about ten minutes later. We jumped into his Charger and headed for Julie's. First, we stopped for a bottle of wine. I never arrived empty handed. I did, however, feel a pang of guilt for not having a new book for Brian.

It turned out that not having a book for Brian didn't matter—he'd finished the entire Monster Hunter series. All that were out, anyway.

"I'm impressed," I said to him as we sat on the back patio.

"It's an awesome series," he beamed. "You were right, Aunt Brit."

"But have you heard the audio versions?" I asked, raising one eyebrow.

Brian gaped at me.

"There's audio versions?!"

I grinned. My heart had never felt fuller. I had all those I truly loved under one roof, and the kid I adored more than killing loved the same stories I did. I was sure it couldn't get any better until I heard Stu and Cody get loud.

I bolted into the house, ready to bodycheck someone. To my surprise, they were acting like football players, fake tackling each other while talking smack.

I jumped between them the first opening I saw.

"TIME OUT!" I held my hands up like a referee would. "Who's the Eagles and who's the Cowboys?"

We all burst out laughing, acknowledging the NFC East rivalry.

"How did you know?" Cody asked.

I breathed again, knowing they were only playing around, but for a minute there I really was in full protection mode.

"Gut feeling," I responded with a smirk. "Besides, no other teams go at it the way you two just were."

Twenty-Two

WHILE IT WASN'T QUITE time for the stalk, I'd decided to at least get the layout of Katie's neighborhood. I knew I wasn't ready for the reality of the kill; I'd screwed myself over when I killed Dario. Then again, I hadn't expected the blow it had dealt me.

I was in the area of Katie's rental when my phone rang. It was Stu. I debated the wisdom of letting him know where I was and what I was doing. Would it set him off, or would he be fine because it was overdue? I truly had no idea given all that he'd been through recently. He did seem okay lately, though.

I let the phone ring a few more times before answering.

"Hey, babe."

"Hey! What are you up to?" he queried.

This isn't normal.

"Oh, not much, just…working. You?"

"Working? From where? I'm home, and you're—Ohhhhh…"

I could hear his grin.

"Yes. *Working.*"

I couldn't help but grin myself. I may not have felt entirely comfortable yet, but I would. And checking out the neighborhood was a step in the right directi on."Well, I'll let you go," he replied.

"No! Wait," I heard myself saying. "Being on the phone with you could help me look like I belong here. Like I'm lost and you live in this neighborhood and are guiding me," I said without thinking.

Stu chuckled.

"Got it."

We chatted the whole time I surveyed the area around where Katie lived. I made mental notes, while Stu told me about his day, and I made no sense about mine. No sense meaning that I was too distracted by taking mental notes to form coherent sentences. Stu knew this and understood. Any other man would have cut me off and hung up or questioned if I were sober.

We continued chatting until I found where Katie was staying. Her car was parked on the driveway of a building that held four apartments. It wasn't very far from my house, either. *Damn, Britney. Could you maybe stop choosing people who live so close?*

This thought I echoed aloud to Stu.

"I can see how that's a bit concerning," he replied thoughtfully. "And yeah, you probably should start paying closer attention to where these people are living. Not that it matters too much in the grand scheme."

I nodded.

"I get that. Maybe it's more paranoia than any-thing."

"That it is," he agreed.

"Okay, well, now that I have a better idea of the neighborhood, I'm headed back. Want me to pick anything up on my way?"

"Nah, just come home. I want you in my arms."

I grinned and stepped on the gas.

"That sounds dreamy," I replied. "I love you."

"Love you, too," he said before ending the call.

I was happy to now have a picture in my head to work with for the planning part of my game. And I was even happier to be going home to Stu. The man who truly understood and loved me for who—and what—I was. I was sure I was the luckiest serial killer alive.

It should have only taken about ten minutes to get home, but there was far too much traffic headed to the base, so it took twice that. I was frustrated by it, but there was nothing I could do. To go through the different neighborhoods would take longer, and all I wanted right then was Stu's strong arms wrapped me while we cuddled on the couch watching anything.

When I finally made it home, I was confused. Stu told me he was home, but his car was missing. It hit me when I opened the garage. He finally did it. I grinned and I shifted into park in the driveway.

I was still grinning when I walked inside and at-tack-hugged Stu.

"What's that for?" he asked half chuckling.

"You finally parked in the garage," I replied, kissing him on the cheek. "It's about damned time you started acting like you live here."

He playfully shoved my shoulder.

"Or maybe I was just tired of you giving me shit about it."

I grinned wider.

"Either way, I win."

Stu just shook his head, smirking.

I laughed as I joined him on the couch. As I sat, I noticed a bottle of wine, a full glass next to it.

"Thanks, babe," I said, reaching for the glass.

Stu beat me to it and plucked the glass from the coffee table, handing it to me. We clinked, my glass to his bottle.

As I sat back, he pressed Play on the show I'd been dying to watch with him. It didn't matter to either of us that I'd already half watched it; I had it on in the background while I worked, and the only episode I truly paid attention to was the finale. It gave me the craziest goose bumps I'd ever experienced. And I'd cried. I knew it would happen again, and I looked forward to it.

Two episodes later, and we were both hungry. Neither one of us felt like cooking, so we went with our default of wings, pizza, and fries. Stu called to place the order, and we went right back to the show. That told me he enjoyed it as much as I did, which made me feel like I was floating on the clouds.

We were halfway in when the doorbell rang. I paused the show and started to get up, but Stu put a hand in front of me.

"I got it."

I eyed him, truly understanding how much this man loved me and would do anything for me. Even something as trivial as getting our delivery order from five feet away.

While he answered the door, I went into the kitchen for plates and napkins. I came back out as he was setting the food on the coffee table. He made a face at me when he saw the plates.

"We can't both eat the pizza or wings from the box," I remarked with a chuckle.

"Who says?" He grinned.

I laughed and shook my head.

We each put pizza, wings, and fries on our plates and got right back to it.

By the time we reached the end of the fourth episode, it was only 6 p.m. There were four episodes left, each of varying length. That didn't deter us, and we plunged ahead.

It was well after ten by the time the series finished, and as hoped, the goose bumps and tears returned. Stu was a little confused by my reaction to that final episode.

"You gotta understand," I started, "The previous episode had my favorite story in it. Then the finale… It just… It was perfection. Masterfully done."

Stu nodded, though I wasn't sure he truly got why it was such a big thing for me.

"You need to read the stories this show is based on," I told him.

"I've read most of them, actually," he replied.

"Well, maybe you need a reread."

He simply looked at me, a smile on his face. Then he stood and started cleaning the remnants of our dinner from the coffee table.

I helped, then started up the stairs after feeding Minion, Stu right behind me.

As we lay in bed, talking softly, staring at the ceiling, Stu wrapped me tight in his arm.

"What's that for?"

"You need to know how much I love you," he replied. "Also, I'm hoping it'll stave off any nightmares."

I snickered.

"Me too, my love. Me. Fucking. Too."

I kissed him goodnight and rolled onto my other side, wriggling around until I got comfortable enough to fall asleep.

My eyes popped open when I heard a knock at the front door.

Twenty-Three

I DIDN'T GET OUT of bed right away, hoping whoever it was had the wrong house. They continued, and I was afraid they'd get desperate enough to ring the bell, so I gingerly slid from the bed. Stu was already in the doorway.

"I've got it. Go back to sleep."

Before I could voice my disagreement, he had vanished, and I heard voices at the bottom of the stairs. I cocked my head closer to the doorway to our bedroom, straining to hear what was going on. Then, Stu called for me.

I threw my robe on and padded down, poking my head around his beefy arm to greet whoever it was.

I was surprised to see Katie standing there looking dejected and sad. *Are people like her capable of true sadness?*

"What's wrong? Do you want to come in?"

She shook her head.

"No, no"—she waved a hand— "I'm not going to be able to make it in tomorrow and wanted you to know."

I screwed my face up in confusion.

"Come again? You could have texted me that." I tried to keep the building anger out of my voice, but she picked up on it.

"I have to go to London tonight. I'm on my way to the airport now and needed the breather."

"Is everything okay?"

"One of my daughters is on holiday from university and asked me to come for the week. I never hear from them anymore and…" She trailed off, one of her eyes starting to water. Then she blinked, and it was gone. "So, I'm going."

I nodded.

"We'll see you when you come back next week. I'll send someone to cover you at the law firm."

"Thank you, Miss Cage." She turned on her heel and walked to her car at the curb.

Stu closed the door and eyed me curiously.

"She didn't even apologize for waking us," he remarked.

I sneered.

"That's because people like her don't see anything wrong with their actions. Very much like Dario…"

We went back upstairs and to sleep.

When Katie came back from her "emergency" trip to England, I sat her down for a one-on-one about boundaries.

"I don't understand," Katie began, "I just got back, and I'm being called into your office? What's happened?"

I cleared my throat.

"You've happened."

She glared at me.

"You can't be showing up at my door at midnight to tell me you're on your way to London for an emergency trip. Especially since it wasn't exactly an emergency."

I glared right back at her, hoping to get her to back down.

She relaxed her face a bit so she didn't look like she was sucking on a lemon. Cat shit maybe, but not a lemon. Then she nodded.

"Next time, text me. And preferably earlier, like before you book your flight," I said.

She nodded. Her hands were on her lap, but I could see that she was having trouble sitting still. It probably made her angry that she couldn't control me and not be having this reprimanding.

Sucks for her.

I stood, reaching my hand out.

To my surprise, Katie took the offered hand and shook it.

"Thanks, Miss Cage. And I apologize for the inconvenience."

She turned and strode out.

I stood there dumbfounded. Narcissists didn't apologize. *That was a lie. She's not sorry for a damned thing.*

I shook it off as a slick smile spread across my face. I'd start the stalk in the next few days.

I'd purposely called this meeting with her at the end of the day so I could be done. Done with her bullshit and done with my day.

Barb and I walked out of the office together and stood in the lot chatting and catching up for another twenty minutes before we both headed home.

Stu was on days, so he'd beaten me home. I was excited about it because today was his first day back on the street.

"How'd it go?" I asked as I walked into the kitchen.

"Good. I'm actually feeling a lot better," he replied. He was at the stove, mixing something on a sheet pan.

It made me happy to hear him say that. I was still concerned but happy.

I walked over to him, glass of iced tea in hand, and peeked around his bicep to see what he was cooking. He spun, grinning, took the tea, then sipped it.

"What are you doing?"

"Well, excuse me," I exaggerated, "I just wanted to know what was for dinner."

Stu's grin remained in place.

"You'll see."

I snort-sighed.

"Fine," I grumbled on my walk back to the fridge for another glass of iced tea.

This time when I opened the fridge, I noticed the lemonade and squealed. *We rarely have lemonade in the house.*

Instead of plain old iced tea, I made myself an Arnold Palmer. And it was heaven. I made a noise of satisfaction that made Stu laugh.

"Sounds like you're having sex," he commented.

"It's not *that* good," I shot back. "But it's good."

We sat and talked about our days until it was time to get the table ready for dinner. Once we'd finished our parmesan-crusted chicken, we cleaned up, and Stu went to the gym, leaving me and Minion to our own devices.

Minion slept on the couch beside me while I studied the satellite view of Google Maps. Katie's apartment was in the center of my screen so I could pan around easier without losing the place.

For the hours Stu was at the gym, I took notes. Mental notes, of course. If I'd written all of them down, I'd definitely have fucked myself over somehow. Well, if I forgot to burn the notes. I wasn't taking the chance. I knew I had more than a few screws loose and could be unreliable. To let that get any worse was unconscionable.

I'd just left the laptop on the kitchen table when Stu came in, smelling like the stench of three sweaty men instead of the one he was. I covered my mouth and nose with one hand and waved in front of my face with the other.

"Aw, come on. I don't smell that—" Stu lifted an arm and smelled himself. "Oh damn! I retract that." The look on his face was priceless.

I nodded, acknowledging his agreement with my actions.

He quickly kissed my cheek then sprinted out of the room and up the stairs.

I was chuckling as I removed my hand from my face when he was gone.

I'd opened the refrigerator door to grab Stu a beer when I heard my phone chirp from the living room. When I picked it up, my face transformed from happy to a whole lot of anger.

Twenty-Four

THE CALLER ID SHOWED the word *Jail*, and I dropped my phone. Whether it was more shock than anger or the other way around, I didn't know. I knew I was shocked, and I knew I was *pissed*.

I went upstairs to talk to Stu before I did something potentially drastic, like throwing a glass against the wall and risk cutting myself or Minion.

He couldn't see my face, thanks to the shower curtain, but he heard my footsteps and somehow knew something was wrong.

"You okay?" he queried.

I huffed out a sigh, crossing my arms over my chest as I leaned against the doorframe for a moment. Then I walked over to the wall next to the toilet, huffing and crossing my arms again.

"No. No I'm not okay," I answered.

"What happened?"

"I got a call from the jail."

Stu poked his head out around the curtain. "You got what?"

I could only nod. I was too angry to say much else. I took a breath, knowing he was waiting for me to say something else—to elaborate. To tell him if I answered and if I did, who it was. I sucked air in through my nose and opened my mouth.

"I didn't answer. For all I know, it was one of the officers on duty."

"Did they leave a message?"

I shrugged. "I don't know."

"Why don't you know? Britney, this is kind of important. If it was John—"

"You think I don't realize that?" I got loud, my voice shrill. "Sorry, that was dramatic. I'm just angry and frustrated, and it's not your fault."

"You're fine, babe," Stu replied.

To me, that meant continue venting. And I did for all of thirty seconds because I had nothing else to say.

"I'll go check my phone to see if whoever it was left a message," I said before using my shoulder blades to push myself off the wall and walk out of the bathroom.

I grumbled to myself all the way back downstairs to pick my phone up from where it landed on the couch when I tossed it. The screen read 1 Missed Call and New Voice Mail.

"Fuck," I said aloud.

I tapped the voice mail icon and listened to the full two-minute message. It was the sergeant on duty, calling to tell me they'd caught John trying to mail me a letter, and when he'd gotten in trouble for it, he tried to call but was blocked somehow. I didn't understand how collect-call blocking worked on that end, and I didn't care. What mattered was that John couldn't contact me. At all.

I waited until I heard the shower turn off before even thinking about telling Stu. I was far too relieved that it wasn't actually John that I sat down on the couch without realizing it. Like the weight had lifted simultaneously and I descended. Or maybe it stayed where it was when I started to sit.

Stu came down a few minutes later, eying me cautiously.

If I was him, I'd be looking at me like I was a bomb about to explode, too.

"So?" he asked, edging between me and the coffee table to sit next to me.

"It was the sergeant on duty," I started. "Apparently, John tried to send me a letter, and when they handed it back and penalized him, he'd tried to call. That was somehow blocked from the jail's end, though."

Stu nodded.

"I don't know how they do that, either."

My head snapped in his direction.

"How did you know I didn't know? That I was wondering how they made that happen?"

"I know you well enough to decipher what you're not saying," he responded simply. Like I was a book that made it easy to read between the lines.

Am I that obvious? I can't be. Maybe it's just to him since we're so much a like yet so different.

I could only shrug and slump my shoulders. Then I leaned forward to grab a glass of wine that wasn't there because I hadn't poured it.

Stu knew exactly what I was doing and stood.

"I was going to grab drinks, but you looked so…off that I wasn't about to put that over you."

He left the room and me on the couch to be alone with my thoughts. That usually turned out to be a bad idea if I was left alone with them for too long. Lucky for me, Stu returned in less than two minutes.

He handed me the bottle and a glass full to just below the brim. I nodded my thanks as I took the glass after setting the bottle on the couch next to me. Then he sat down, beer in hand.

I gulped my glass three or four times until it was empty while staring at the floor. Stu remained quiet the whole time, though I felt his eyes on me.

I didn't know how much time had passed between finishing the glass and grabbing the bottle next to me, but I realized I was twisting the cap from the bottle and snapped back to reality. I looked over at Stu and forced a smile.

Stu shook his head.

"Don't do that," he said. "I know better."

I nodded, somehow back in space.

"I don't know why I'm so fucked up lately. I've been seeing Ben weekly, and we've been making real progress. He even gave me homework that I've been doing." I shook my head. "But sometimes I'm rattled easier than most. And I *hate* it. So much."

I dropped my head, feeling like the worst fiancée, like I wasn't in a position to be anyone's significant other.

Stu reached out, gently touching my thigh.

"You're not the person you're thinking you are. I promise. It's not a phase, but it's part of healing," he said.

My head shot up.

"How would you know? You're not healed, and you haven't tried," I spat.

Stu remained stoic as I lashed out.

"I did try. I wasn't strong enough to keep going, to do the work," he admitted.

For once, my face didn't shift into anything. It was just blank. I had no words. Just then, something in my head snapped like a rubber band that had been pulled and let go.

"You're full of shit." I scoffed. "You're the kind of person who doesn't stop until it's better."

Stu shook his head slowly.

"I'm not, though." He took my hand and caressed it, not looking up at me.

"I act that way, sure, but the truth is I've never been strong enough to keep facing my demons and hurt until I've won. I give up every time." He sniffed. "It's embarrassing admitting this to you, but I don't want to hide things from you, either. You're about to be my wife, and that means more than my pride."

Now it was my turn to sniffle. The difference was that tears flowed from my eyes, while Stu's just watered a little bit.

I cracked a small smile and joked. "Just me, huh?"

Stu cocked his head a tiny bit before what my joke meant clicked in his head. Then he smiled a bit.

"You don't always have to make jokes, you know," he said.

"Oh, but I do," I replied grinning. "How else would we get through? If not for sarcasm and dark humor, you and I would be screwed."

Twenty-Five

THERE WAS A STOP sign about forty feet away, and my foot was already on the brake pedal when something shot between my front bumper and the rear of the car in front of me. I pressed down as hard as I needed to, lurching my Jeep to a stop. I took a deep breath and saw a kid around the age of ten bolt between us like he was chasing something. I took another breath to steady myself as the car in front of me took their turn.

I looked all around trying to make sure I wasn't about to kill something I didn't intend to. When I was satisfied, I turned left.

Two miles down the road, I saw her, so I pulled against the curb where I could see her walking in the same direction I was driving.

She walked alone, and it seemed to me she didn't even have earbuds in. Her head only moved as it should for a brisk pace. No dancing or head bopping, nothing. *What kind of weirdo is she?*

She wasn't a weirdo; she was a narcissist. There was a difference. There were probably psychologists who wanted to study her, but she'd never make it that far. She'd met me first.

She was walking on the sidewalk and hung a right, presumably in the direction of where she was living. I waited a few minutes before starting the engine and following.

I reached the corner, and she was only six or seven houses down, so I decided not to turn down that road. Instead, I drove down to the next street and made a right. I reached the stop sign, and when I looked right, I saw Katie on the opposite side of the intersection. An evil grin cut my lips, and I crept the block to have a better vantage point.

Every time Katie crossed an intersection, I'd creep up to the block behind her. I wasn't as slick as I'd wanted to be, but I was having fun. It reminded me of those old episodes of *Looney Tunes*. I should have done laps and driven all over to reinforce my knowledge of the neighborhood instead of risking her seeing me. But I also needed to learn her routines.

So I continued following her until she went inside her apartment. I waited another thirty minutes to make sure she didn't go somewhere else before taking my leave. Of course, I wondered if today was a normal thing or not, and knew I'd need to follow her on other days of the week to verify her patterns.

Stu had the day off, so he was home when I got there. I giggled when I saw that his car had been moved from the garage to up against the curb where he used to park.

Inside the house, Stu was lounging on the couch, shirtless. Once I'd realized that, I bit my lower lip, craving something.

"Mm," I moaned as I walked by.

"Hm?"

I pulled my shirt off as I walked around the end of the couch. He wasn't really paying attention, which made what I did next that much more fun.

"Hey, babe," he greeted, placing a hand on my thigh. That was exactly what I needed to happen, especially that he still wasn't looking at me.

I lifted my other leg up and hoisted myself onto the couch on top of him. He turned his head, his cheeks flushed, a look of happy surprise in his eyes and on his face. He sat up and kissed me. From that moment, everything felt like magic.

I came back downstairs around five, owing to dehydration and having worked up a hunger. Stu came down as I was poking around the fridge and freezer, trying to decide what to do for dinner. When I closed the double doors of the fridge, I jumped. Stu was standing there with a grin on his face.

"What the fuck, man," I asked with a chuckle. "Don't do that to me."

Stu let out a giggle.

"That's exactly why I did it," he said, opening one of the doors to grab a beer.

"How can you not be as dehydrated as I am?" I asked, pouring a glass of water and adding lemon juice to it.

"I am," he responded.

I could only shake my head and let out the tiniest of chuckles before trying not to chug or choke on my water.

"Did you find anything in there?" Stu asked, nodding his head toward the fridge.

"Not really," I muttered. "Nothing I'm in the mood for, anyway."

"So no meat to make burgers?"

I shook my head.

"Then we order out or *go* out," he stated.

I shrugged.

"I'm good with ordering out. Don't want to go out; hell, I can barely walk normal," I said, waddling over to, and then past, him. I paused next to him for a split second to kiss his cheek and whisper into his ear. "Thank you for that."

Stu came into the living room, where I'd plopped down onto the couch.

"Do you know what you want?" he asked as he sat down beside me.

"Where are you ordering from?"

"I was thinking Outback or maybe trying Brick House."

"I'll give Brick House a shot. Some place we haven't had yet."

Stu handed me his phone so I could choose what I wanted, then entered his selections. A few more taps later, and Stu grinned.

"Thirty minutes," he said.

"Guess you'll need to put some more clothes on," I noted with a smirk.

"Bah, it's being delivered," he replied.

It's a challenge to keep my hands off you right now, and you're not putting more clothes on?

"It's a challenge to keep my hands off you right now, and you're not putting more clothes on?" The words came out of my mouth before I knew that I'd thought them first.

Stu's face flushed.

"The feeling is mutual."

He sat on the couch next to me, and we just stared at each other. Not in that sort of showdown look, but one of pure love and adoration, laced with lust and greed.

I snapped out of it thanks to the pangs of dehydration still hitting me. I plucked my glass from the table and finished it in two gulps, then stood to get more. Stu stood with me but headed for the stairs.

"Change your mind?" I called after him.

He didn't respond. More like if he did, I couldn't hear him because he was upstairs, and I was in the kitchen. I refilled my glass and poured him one whether he wanted it or not.

We met in the living room, and when Stu noticed a second glass on the table, he chuckled.

"Thanks, Brit. I guess you really do love me."

I grinned and pressed Play on a movie we'd just added to our list. We were about ten minutes into it when the doorbell rang. Stu bolted up and to the door as I paused the movie and went to the kitchen.

Stu joined me, and we divvied up the fries after figuring out which burger was whose. The wings we left in their container to pick at as we wanted.

"This can't continue to be our norm," I commented on our walk to the living room.

"I know," Stu agreed, "I feel like I have to work harder every day at the gym."

I snarled.

"Don't remind me that I haven't been there in forever. Shit! We forgot drinks."

I jogged into the kitchen and came back with an armful of beers, knowing Stu would down two in his first few bites. I'd drink more, too, but while eating wings. These were our habits.

By the time the movie ended, we were both stuffed and exhausted. On our way up to bed, I vowed to start jogging every morning again. It would be easier, too, now since I was working from home. I had no reason to rush the jog, and I didn't have to get ready once I got back because I had nowhere to go except the kitchen or patio.

Twenty-Six

I MADE GOOD ON my promise to myself to start jogging again. Not that time mattered anymore, but my route only took about forty minutes, which was what it had taken me the last time I jogged. Before I'd killed Dario.

It felt good to be hitting the concrete sidewalks again; I never realized how good it felt except when I was jogging off a bad mood or anger. Sure, my knees might hurt a little afterward, but the rest of my body felt amazing. I was sure there was no way of working out that would feel like this or even come close. As I chugged water in my kitchen, I recalled Julie talking about some app that was less painful on the joints and took half the time of one of my jogs.

I walked over to my phone on the table and texted her.

I set the phone back down and refilled my glass. It chimed as soon as I stepped away. Glass in hand, I snatched the phone and headed upstairs to shower before starting my day. I unlocked the screen and opened Julie's response.

It's called BetterMe. I do the wall Pilates and ignore the eating plan.

There's an eating plan, too?! Nah, I'm good without that nonsense :D I'll check it out, though. Or do you get something if you refer me to it? If you do, send me that referral link.

I damn near tripped up the last step, so I locked my screen and paid more attention to where I was walking. Once in the bathroom, I set the glass on the counter and unlocked my screen just as it chimed again.

It was the referral link I' asked for. I tapped it, installed the app, and entered my card info.

If Julie said it worked, I was happy to give it a go. Besides, I'd seen it in a few of the magazines I read, and they'd all given it stellar reviews. Though I now suspected that *those* bitches followed the eating plan, too. How anyone could do that—unless they had food allergies or something—was beyond my understanding. If it tasted good, I was going to eat it. Didn't matter what it was. Most of the time, I only asked if I *really* liked it, anyway. Maybe I'd seen that temple movie where they ate monkey brains one too many times.

Once I'd finished paying for the workout program, I picked out leggings and a T-shirt for the day and showered the sweat and sand from my skin. I hadn't even jogged on the sand—I hated that I couldn't get the proper footing on dry sand and never wanted to get close to the water enough to get wet feet—but Bayshore *was* right along the bay.

After I got out, I dressed and got to work. It was a Monday, and Mondays flew for me. Before I knew it, the day was over, and Stu was home.

I told him about the app as he was getting ready for the gym.

"How about try it while I'm lifting?" he suggested.

I nodded.

"I like that idea."

Stu left and I got to it.

I wasn't aware that I'd need quite a bit of empty wall space, but I found it in the guest room. I even had the empty floor space required. Though some parts I had a difficult time understanding how they were called Pilates when they were just modified exercises. Either way, I was liking the workout.

I'd showered and gotten into bed before Stu got home and was reading when he came up.

He smiled at me as he walked over to my side of the bed to kiss me.

"How was it?" He asked.

"I was about to tell you, but you kinda beat me to it," I replied. "It was surprisingly good."

Stu grinned.

"I wish I could say the same. It was good, just not surprisingly so."

I shoved him playfully.

"Well, I can smell how well it went, so how about you get a shower and join me under the covers?" I arched a brow and bit my lower lip as I ended.

Stu said nothing and started removing his clothes en route to the bathroom.

I knew neither one of us had the energy for sex right now, but being playful was too much fun and could set the stage for us to tease each other tomorrow.

As predicted, Stu was too worn out. I couldn't blame him because I was too. Besides, what was I just saying to myself about trying to get to bed at a more reasonable hour?

I'd started taking time daily to follow Katie and learn her ways and routines. She was as pre-dictable as she was not, for whatever sense that made. Most days she'd walk the same route. Some days, however, she'd walk to Starbucks and back, which was over three miles one way.

Sure, I jogged that far and back, but that was different, right? It had to be. Something like my fitness goals were…better or something.

It went on like that for weeks, almost a full month. Until one day, she just stopped walking. Something in my gut was saying she'd realized she was being followed, so I stopped hanging around her neighborhood.

Instead, I'd sit out on a main road and follow her to and from the legal office she was temping at. If kidnapping her on her way to either place *had* to happen, at least I knew which way she drove. But I didn't want to have to ditch her car as well as her body. Cars could get costly if I kept paying that guy at the junkyard.

Twenty-Seven

FOR THE NEXT FEW weeks, I'd sit in the garage Katie parked in, waiting for her to finish for the day so I might be able to cobble together a plan if I had to. I was still against catching her stopping off somewhere after work. Besides, she only ever went to Publix.

"What a fucking wet noodle," I muttered. I was grumpy that this was what I'd resorted to. I needed something better for kidnapping her. I *needed* to catch her while out for one of her walks.

After following her three blocks from her house, I went home and whined to Stu.

I finished my rant, and Stu looked at me, a twinkle in his eye like I'd never seen before.

"I go back on nights next week," he said. "You can watch her place all night, if you want. I can make sure you don't get caught by any other uni than me."

I could feel my own eyes gleaming as the face-eating grin spread across my face. I leaped at him, wrapping him in an attack hug.

"You're a fucking genius!"

Stu nodded and patted the back of my shoulder.

"Brit…seriously…loosen up… Choking…"

"Oh!" I unhooked my arms entirely, spreading them wide. "I'm so sorry! Are you okay?"

Stu nodded, a hand on his throat, the other hanging at his side.

"I'm good," he replied hoarsely.

I was afraid to touch him then, so I held my hands about an inch away from his shoulders.

"I'm so sorry, babe. Can I get you some water?"

Stu shook in what I thought might be an adverse reaction to the thought of drinking water. But he nodded.

"Thanks."

I moved as fast as I could to get him that glass of water. I handed it to him before attempting to sit. I'd probably have dropped it or worn it; I was slightly shaky myself from almost accidentally rendering my fiancé unconscious.

We sat there, unmoving, unspeaking, for what felt like hours. Truly, it was only a few minutes, but for the first time in a long time, I was at a loss for words. The last time I couldn't speak was the night Stu proposed.

Something else to tell Ben about, I suppose. "Yeah, so I almost knocked Stu out by hugging him too hard." That would get a laugh out of him, though.

Those thoughts reminded me...

I glanced at my watch and practically jumped from the couch.

"I hate to do this after I almost killed you, but I gotta go."

Stu looked at me quizzically.

"Ben," I said before kissing his forehead, grabbing my purse and keys, and running out the door.

The traffic… Well, it was normal. And total shit. But somehow I made it to Ben's office with two minutes to spare. I burst through the door, apologizing for being late. But Ben's office door was closed, which meant he likely didn't even hear me.

I let out an audible "whoosh," grateful that his appointment before me showed, and plopped down on a chair. Exactly two minutes later, Ben's door opened. A woman exited, sunglasses on her face in a lame attempt to obscure her identity. The joke was on her because I truly couldn't have cared less who she was or why she was there.

The woman hadn't even left the lobby before I stood and walked into Ben's office, not bothering to wait for him to call me in. They'd known I was there from the second I walked in. They'd heard the door chime and my loud apology.

Ben didn't need to say anything—merely look at me and nod—for me to know it was my turn to start talking. And I did, opening with a tone of borderline hysteria that I'd almost killed the only man who truly loved me for *me*.

He held a hand up.

"Hang on," he said between gulps of air, "how did you almost kill him? And why?"

I was frustrated and it showed. My hands were fidgety, my heels tapped the floor, and I felt the look on my face and its ability to melt plastic.

"I attack-hugged him. Apparently, my shoulder was pressed into his throat, so it wasn't like I'm strong enough to do that."

Ben snickered and swallowed whatever words he'd thought better of speaking. Then he cleared his throat.

"And why did you *attack-hug* him?"

Shit. Why didn't I realize he'd ask that? Fuck, fuck, fuckity FUCK! Think fast, Brit.

"He decided to surprise me with tickets to Universal. Park-hopper passes, to be precise. You know how much I love that place," I lied. "I haven't been there in so long."

"That was sweet of him," Ben commented. "Are you going for the day or making a weekend out of it?"

"I think day because Stu has work the day before or something. I don't really know."

Lame, Britney. Fucking LAME.

Ben snorted.

"That was lame, Brit," he said, echoing my own thoughts quite well.

I chuckled in spite of myself.

"You know how hard it is for me to admit I don't know; I always *have* to know. I'm not a control freak, or I am. But Stu seems to be the only person who can truly surprise me and get away with it."

Ben nodded his agreement.

"I've noticed that." He cleared his throat. "If you don't mind my saying, we've known each other a long time. I've never seen you like this. So complete-ly trusting and adoring of someone."

I snickered.

"Thanks?"

Ben smiled at me.

"I mean it as a compliment, so you're welcome. Seriously, you're not the cold-hearted bitch you think you are. At least not when it comes to those who hold a place in—or piece of—your heart."

That stung, and I physically recoiled, panic attack in full effect.

Ben hopped the four feet across the floor and sat next to me, speaking calm and low, as if cooing a baby back to sleep. It was calming enough to take my focus off the lack of air in my lungs and racing heart.

"Thank you," I mumbled.

When I was breathing easily again, Ben shifted back to his chair, asking questions to get me to think about the responses and how to handle the emotions that came with those responses. Sometimes I hated therapy, and this was one of those times. I also appreciated it. Without Ben, I'd still be a dumpster fire of a person, feeling those emotions I'd felt when I killed Dario.

Now, though, I felt the closest to myself as I had since before even dating Dario. Hell, I was pretty sure I was an *improved* version of her. Except I found myself feeling like a failure of a daughter to Joe. I'd spoken to my bio-dad more than him in the past month.

When the session was over, I got in my Jeep, intending to call Joe. An incoming call stopped me in my tracks.

Twenty-Eight

THE SCREEN ON MY dashboard read *Jail* again. This time I answered.

"Hu-llo?" It was exaggerated, and I was annoyed, and I didn't care who on the other end heard it.

"Miss Cage? This is Sergeant Bob Smith at the Hillsborough County Jail," he said.

"And? What do you want?"

"John Sweet really wants to talk to you," he began, "He's been trying to send you letters and call you, knowing he's blocked from both."

"Okay, well, don't you read the letters anyway?"

"No, ma'am, we don't. But we do pay attention to who they're addressed to. We only scan the incoming mail for things like contraband."

"Okay, well let's suppose I actually *want* to know what he has to say? What are my options to do that?"

"Well, you could come for a visit, or I can hold the last letter he tried to send, and you can come pick it up," he offered.

FUCK! What am I supposed to do? I kinda want to know what that moron has to say for himself, though I don't expect any level of remorse. He's prob-

ably just calling me a killer some more or something. But…what could it hurt?

Curiosity was about to kill this particular cat.

"I'll come get the letter. Can I do it now? I'm in my car anyway."

The sergeant agreed to meet me outside once I arrived for the letter. He asked that I call him when I pulled on property. I agreed and we hung up.

I pressed the talk button on my steering wheel, and my car chimed.

"Call Stu."

Three seconds later, a ringing phone played through all my speakers.

"Hey, babe," Stu answered.

I told him all the sergeant had told me, then let him know I was on my way to the jail.

"Why not swing home and come get me? I'll go with you," he offered.

"I'm already on 75," I replied. "About to get off at MLK now, actually."

There was a moment of silence on the other end.

"Already!"

I glanced at the clock on the touch screen.

"Oh…yeah. I guess I may have been driving a little over the limit," I ceded.

I turned onto Falkenburg as Stu and I ended our conversation with me agreeing to call him the second I left the jail.

As I turned into the parking lot, I called the number the sergeant had given me and let him know where I was parking. He came out to meet me—or was it? The way he eyed me up and down made me feel this old perv had something else in mind. Maybe this asshole would get lucky. Maybe I'd put him on my list, too.

We discussed that John wasn't allowed to contact me, and why, as he handed me the letter. I thanked him and said I'd rather read the letter at home. He seemed to understand, though I could see the disappointment on his face that he wouldn't know what it contained. I daresay he was itching to have things done to John.

I turned to leave but twisted back to Bob.

"Can I ask you something?"

He nodded. "Sure can."

"What do you have against Sweet that you seem to be champing at the bit to get him?"

Bob gave me a deer-in-the-headlights look.

"I won't tell anyone," I promised. Whether I kept that promise depended on how this man in front of me answered, but he didn't need to know that.

He bowed his head and thought for a moment.

"He's given all of us in uniform who swore to protect this county and city a bad name by breaking into your house. He made it worse by continuing to shout to anyone who will listen that you're a killer. If he had proof, that would be one thing, but he's got nothing other than a 'weird feeling' as he puts it." He mimicked John's voice when he said that.

I held back a snicker—the sergeant's impression was spot on.

"I don't know what his problem with you is, Miss Cage, but he's delusional."

"Don't need to tell me. I'm the one who shot him, remember?" I replied. I stuck out a hand, and we shook. "Thanks, Sergeant Smith. I appreciate it. Just don't let him know I have the letter, all right?"

He grunted.

"Never. And you're welcome. It was nice meeting you, even under these circumstances," he said, eying the ring on my left hand then stepping back before turning around and walking back into the building.

I hopped back into my Jeep and called Stu. I was around twenty minutes from home, given the time of day.

"Okay. Drive safe. I love you," he said.

"I love you, too," I replied before hanging up.

I wanted to pull over on the ride home to read the letter, but Stu was already expecting me so that was out. I'd have to read it there, and he'd likely want to know what it said. I wasn't sure I wanted to share it, but I also knew I could trust that he wouldn't judge me for anything Sweet had to say. Even if it was the truth.

When I walked in the front door, Stu was nowhere to be seen.

"Babe?" I called as I took my shoes off and set them on the stand.

"Out here," came his distant reply. He was out on the patio.

I padded out there, opening the letter as I did. Stu smiled seeing me walk out, distracted as I was. He patted his leg, and I sat down, hugging and kissing him.

I pulled the letter back into my line of sight and began reading aloud without realizing it. Stu leaned his head back and listened.

When I finished, the two of us looked at each other, grinning before bursting into hysterics. John was very clear that he "knew" I was a killer; that I killed Alex. He also knew I killed Brody, the sisters, Shae, and everyone else. He didn't bother to tell me how he knew all of the victims since not all had made the news.

"And here I was thinking no one believed him. But someone was feeding him info from the inside, right?" I looked at Stu.

"Not necessarily," Stu replied.

"What do you mean?"

"He could be reading the obituaries."

"Son of a…"

Stu nodded.

"I must really think I'm invincible," I muttered, disappointed in myself.

Stu sat up, his eyes boring into mine.

"You never thought that. I can see that in your eyes. I hear it when we talk. That's hope, not belief. That's you essentially lying to yourself. But you've got me now. Which means that lessens your chances of being caught."

I absorbed his words, my emotions threatening to take over.

"Stop. I see what's about to happen," Stu said.

I hung my head, unable to deny anything at that moment. The floodgates opened, and Stu wrapped me in his arms. This was why he'd said stop.

I let it all out for a few minutes on his shoulder. He caressed my hair as I cried, trying to soothe me, knowing the only thing that would work right then was to let me cry it all out. And when I had, I picked my head up and kissed his cheek.

"Thank you," I whispered.

Stu kissed me back, his way of acknowledging my appreciation.

I stared at the letter, wondering why John thought it important to let me know he knew these things. I mean, yeah, I *did* kill those people. But why did I need to know he knew when no one believed him?

"Okay, so, what difference does it make to me that he knows when I also know that no one believes him and everyone thinks he's crazy? What does this accomplish for him?"

Stu pondered that for a few minutes, as did I. I almost gave myself a headache thinking about it. My phone rang, pulling me from getting too much deeper.

I picked it up. It was Sergeant Smith.

Twenty-Nine

"Hi, Sergeant. What can I do for you?"

He rambled some sort of greeting like he wasn't calling about something vaguely important.

"Well, I'd like to let you know that John's in the infirmary," he said.

"I don't particularly care," I responded. "Why did you really call?"

Stu eyed me and tried not to laugh. I turned the phone to speaker.

"I wanted to know what the letter said," Bob answered.

"Nothing much," I said, "Just his usual bullshit that he knows I'm a killer."

Bob scoffed, and Stu snickered with a hand over his mouth so Bob didn't hear him.

"Well, Miss Cage, I know no one believes him, and I apologize for him continuing his nonsense."

"Thanks, but it's not your job to apologize for him. Was there anything else you needed?"

"No, ma'am. Have a good night."

"Thanks, you, too."

I hung up before he did, and for once didn't wonder why he'd hesitated. I simply didn't care. Stu, on the other hand, had something to say about it.

"He wanted to ask you out."

I threw my head back and cackled.

"Ohhhh no. You should have seen his face when he noticed my ring," I said when I'd stopped laughing.

Stu chuckled, but I could tell he didn't think that would stop this guy. I didn't either and knew better than to put myself in a position where he could ask me out.

"If he calls me again, I'll call his boss," I said.

Stu nodded.

"Good idea."

I stood, picking the letter up off the table where I'd dropped it.

"What are you going to do with it?" Stu asked.

A wicked grin opened on my face.

"What else do we do with evidence?" I responded darkly.

Stu chuckled, knowing what I was referring to.

I walked into the kitchen and opened the cabinet I kept the plates in. I took one out and rummaged in a drawer for a lighter.

Back outside, I set the plate on the table, lit the lighter, and held the flame to the letter. Once it caught, I held it, staring at it, getting lost in the flame, thinking about what fire did to a human body.

Stu tapped my arm and nodded at the letter, the flames licking higher, almost touching my fingers. I dropped it on the plate to finish burning.

The fire was a turn-on for me, and Stu knew it. He sat up and kissed me hard. I kissed him back harder while the letter burned itself out.

Not that it mattered—we were too busy to notice or care. There was no chance of it catching anything else, either, since there were no embers.

We stumbled through the kitchen, pulling at each other's clothes, until Stu picked me up. I wrapped my legs around him, and he carried me into the living room. I'd hoped we'd have kitchen sex, but the couch would suffice, too.

After we finished and got dressed, I decided to follow Katie some more. That bitch needed to go, and I was tired of being patient. The issue was that Stu didn't leave for work for another three hours.

He saw the look in my eyes, the glimmer of the impending kill, and knew what I was thinking.

"Wait," he said. "I know it's difficult, but let me get to work first."

I nodded.

"In that case, I'm going to take a nap." I shooed him down the couch so I could lie down fully, my feet on his lap.

"What about—"

I waved him off.

"I'll deal with it before I leave to stalk."

I flipped through Netflix until Stu had me stop and turn something he was interested in on. I shrugged, not truly caring since I was half-asleep. You're *like a man, Brit. You cum and then pass out.* That thought made me snicker quietly, but Stu caught it.

"What's that?"

I told him and he grinned, shaking his head.

"You are," he agreed.

I smiled, eyes still closed, and fell asleep.

I was awakened by Stu's gentle touch on my arm. He'd gotten up off the couch and kneeled on the floor, lightly squeezing my arm.

I groaned. I didn't particularly want to wake up, but I knew I had to. Besides, knowing I'd be following Katie again made me grin even if I was half-asleep.

"I'm going to get ready for work," Stu told me after I sat up.

I nodded, rubbing my eyes.

It took me a few more minutes before I was awake enough to get up off the couch and walk up-stairs. When I got into the bedroom, Stu was towel-ing off from his shower. We smiled at each other and kissed, headed in opposite directions.

Inside the closet, I double-checked my bag. Everything I needed was there, right down to the duct tape and ketamine already in a syringe. I smiled as I zipped it back up and stood.

I grabbed a pair of black pants and a black top. I may not have been kidnapping her tonight, but it was better to be less noticeable in case I had to get out of my car anywhere near her house or walking route.

My bag was in my hand as I turned to walk out of the closet. Stu was walking in wearing his uniform pants and vest on top of an undershirt. I grinned and pulled a uniform shirt from a hanger, handing it to him. He took it, nodding his thanks, something else on his mind.

"Wait for me to let you know I'm on the street before you leave," he said.

I heaved a sigh.

"Okay."

Stu chuckled and put a hand on my shoulder.

"I'm proud of you."

"For what?"

"I know you wanted to say 'fine' all grumpy-like."

It was my turn to chuckle.

Stu put his shirt on, letting me out of the closet with my bag before buttoning up.

Not that I needed to go through it again or sort or repack, but I plopped the bag on the bed and checked it again. Because I was neurotic or because I needed to be sure, I couldn't tell. Either way, everything I needed if I were to take her tonight was there.

I went into the garage and threw the bag into my back seat. As I walked back into the house, Stu was ready to leave.

"What are you thinking? Thirty minutes?" I asked, kissing his cheek.

"Figure an hour, but I'll call you once I'm in the patrol car."

I nodded.

"Be safe," I said as he walked to the front door.

He looked back at me. "Always," he replied, blowing me a kiss.

My heart always stopped for a minute when Stu left for duty. I never knew if this time would be the last. That was the way of loving a cop.

Thirty

I'D BEEN PACING FOR what felt like hours when Stu called. The pre-shift meeting ran over because they were welcoming Stu back. I thought that was odd considering he'd been back for weeks at this point; they were all on days together the previous weeks.

"Whatever," I said shrugging like he could see me. "Can I leave now?"

He knew I was ready to go, that I might even want to take her tonight. I did, of course, but I wasn't going to risk not being fully ready or without a plan. I wasn't fully ready, not mentally, just angry and spiteful.

Then again, I could take her tonight. She had no one to miss her, and I could keep her for days before killing and dumping her body. The choices were all too much to think about, and I wasn't about to discuss them over the phone with Stu.

"Meet me when you're there?" I asked.

"Of course," he replied.

We said our goodbyes, and I jumped in the Jeep, grin on my face. Tonight could very well be Katie's last night of freedom.

My Jeep was noticeable, yet no one seemed to care. It was as though I should have been in that neighborhood. Lots of people were out walking; the weather was perfect for it.

I snorted in annoyance that so many people were out and about. I knew that if I'd tried to take her tonight, it could be the most dangerous thing I'd ever done. And I was willing to risk it, provided I could find the proper opening to inject the ketamine.

Stu called about the same time I snorted.

"Meet me closer to the Bayshore gate of the base."

"Good, there's a lot of people out tonight," I replied disappointed.

We met up a block or so away from the gate, taking up a whole street since they were narrow. Stu's car faced one way, mine another. We chatted for a little while, discussing how I could pull this off tonight if I even wanted to. I didn't, but it was also potentially opportune, so long as Katie was still out after the majority had gone inside.

As luck would have it, that's precisely how things played out.

Stu was patrolling the neighborhood, making sure any people were far enough away. I had him on the Jeep's Bluetooth, so I could hear him as I drove. When I'd found a good spot to leave it, I put an earbud in and switched the phone output. I hopped out and silently walked behind Katie.

She must have sensed me because about a quarter block after I'd gotten out of my Jeep, she turned around, almost knowing someone was behind her. I didn't bother trying to hide or duck out of her line of sight. Instead, I stood there and waved.

"Hi, Katie!" I called. "It's such a beautiful night out, and I thought I'd take a walk."

She eyed me skeptically.

"You live around here?" she questioned.

"I do! A couple blocks down Bayshore." I pointed.

She nodded her head to the side, asking me to join her. "Come on."

I grinned, my hand gripping the ketamine syringe in my pocket. She had no idea what was about to hit her.

We walked and talked, about everything and nothing of importance. I knew she was lying about most things she'd said about her family. Her husband had emailed me, and we'd talked at length about why Katie was here instead of England with her girls.

Nothing that man told me surprised me, and I'd let him know. Meanwhile, he'd informed me they'd been married over twenty years, and all of it still surprised him.

"I know these things all too well," I told him, "I may not have married it, but I was with someone like her for about two years and learned quickly the damage they can do."

Of course, I was speaking of Dario.

We'd talked a little longer, me not letting on that she might go missing, might not turn up. He'd seemed to know all along that something would happen and that Katie would never make it back. And he was more than okay with it.

Truthfully speaking, I was okay with him seeing that; the truth of things that weren't exactly my truth.

The call had ended, and I'd begun planning Katie's demise.

Here I was, walking with her while she talked at length about her ex-husband, the one I'd spoken to. I may not have known him the way she did, but I did know he wasn't the things she'd accused him of being. Sure, he was a coward; he was a man. In my experience, they all were.

But she'd successfully controlled him for so long… He never knew until it was too late. Poor guy.

Then again, I'd never realized it with Dario until it was too late. Then it turned into something far too late for him.

Katie, though, thought she knew it all. It was the look on her face when I stabbed her in the neck with my syringe that she realized she knew nothing.

Thirty-One

I GENTLY LED HER to the ground, then taped her wrists, feet, and mouth. Carrying her to the back of my Jeep sucked, but I did and threw her limp body into the tiny cargo space. I stared at her as she lay there, pathetic. Like no one had ever truly cared for her.

"Ah, but you're so wrong," I muttered. "They all loved you until they saw the truth of you."

I closed the cargo door, a slick grin on my face. She'd never realize until I had her locked to the lift with the chain.

And that's just where she came to, me sitting on a chair, my back to her until I heard her speak.

"What's going on? Who are you? What do you want?" She cried, pulling at her chains.

I twisted around on my chair, the grin on my face similar to that of the Joker, but more…human. More evil.

I stood, knife in hand, waving it to and fro as I spoke.

"Oh good! You're awake," I started.

"What do you—Oh. It's you," she said, recoiling when she recognized me.

My grin swallowed my face, like those from all the horror movies. And I wasn't hiding anything now.

"Yes, it's me," I replied. "You're stuck where you are. And you're screwed. So, Katie, tell me, why did your ex deserve what you did to him? The lies, the cheating… Better yet, why did your children deserve that? The way you spoke to them, how they were mere pawns in your game… Tell me, how do you give birth to something only to hate it?"

Her face twisted into something I could recognize. Was it anger, hatred, sadness? I didn't know, but she spat in my direction. I threw my head back and cackled.

"You think that's going to affect me?" I laughed louder. "Try again, cunt." I spat in her face.

Katie began to cry, making me laugh harder.

"You're so full of shit.""No," she sobbed, "I have two teenage girls… Please let me go!"

She was trying to play a game she expected me to be none the wiser of.

"Oh, Katie," I sighed, tapping my knife against my cheek. "Do you think me so oblivious? Do you think I'm that…*stupid*?" I was a villain of the highest caliber…or maybe not as high as her. But I was dark and devious. And my fiancé was a cop, which meant my back was covered. The venom of my words made her shrink a little.

"I'll have you know…your ex and I have spoken a few times. And I've talked to your girls. None of them want you around. Your girls know what you are and have only been playing the game until they started university. Now that they're there, they don't need or want you. They know their father is the only one who actually loves them," I said, walking around her.

She writhed against the chains holding her wrists above her head. She screamed at me.

I laughed harder.

"Stop. You know as well as I do they're smarter than you give them credit for; they *know* what you are."

Her eyes shot daggers at me, and I tilted my head to one side.

"Give it a rest. I'm worse that you could ever imagine." The smile that split my face gave her a glimpse of the pure evil inside of me she could see on the outside.

I resembled Harley Quinn at that moment—the tip of the knife I held scratching my cheek, my eyes appearing as though they were unable to focus...

"Tell me," I said, "what did he do to deserve you running around on him with his BEST FRIEND?"

Katie's eyes went wide, her face taught.

I laughed again.

"Stop that. You'll make yourself look even older than you already do."

That earned me a sour face, like she'd just sucked a lemon.

I was at the point I couldn't help myself; I laughed until it hurt.

Katie wasn't sure how to react to anything, so she pulled and twisted and pulled some more against her chains. Her wrists and arms started to bleed, amusing me. When she finally realized there was nothing else she could do and slumped against the lift, I felt a slight twinge of pity. Just that tiny bit.

I squatted down, the tip of the knife against her cheek now, a delirious smile on mine.

"See, you misunderstand," I said to her. "I take great pride in my villainy. And to be honest, you're not all that worth it. But also, you are. That said…" I ran the tip of the blade against her cheek, drawing a thin line of red.

She tried to wriggle free, making me laugh again. I held the knife tighter against her face. Her movements severed another line in her skin.

The toothy grin on my face was now creepier than anything she'd ever seen, creepier than anything I'd ever seen.

I stood, as did Katie. She tried to call me out on who knew what. As soon as she began to yell, I shifted the blade to her chest, letting her know in no uncertain terms that if she'd kept it up, I'd carve her heart out while she still drew breath. She must have thought I was kidding…

"You're so insecure, Britney Cage!"

For the last time, I threw my head back, cackled, and plunged the knife into her heart. The blood gurgled for a few seconds before coming out of her mouth. I pulled down, bringing the knife lower into her rib cage. It wasn't as easy as the movies made it look. Au contraire, it took more strength than I knew I had to break more ribs.

The deed was done, and Katie was dead. I pulled my phone from my pocket. When the line was answered, all I said was "It's done," and the line disconnected.

The garage door opened and closed, the silhouette of a person barely visible. That person wrapped an arm around my waist and kissed me.

I pressed my cheek into his lips, feeling the love and shared hatred of those who treated their children as insignificant.

Katie lay dead on the dirt floor of the shop. Stu and I stood there, looking at her as though she might still move.

"This isn't a movie," Stu said. "But if a headshot is necessary—" He handed me his weapon. Not his police issue, but his personal.

I gripped the gun, knowing I wouldn't need it—knowing I'd split her heart in two actual pieces, and grinned.

Stu unlocked her chains and wrapped her in a contractor bag for me, like a gift. I kissed him hard.

"Thank you," I said to him.

He nodded and helped me lift her into the back of my Jeep.

"Meet you at the dock," he said.

"But the boat—"

"Is waiting for us," he finished.

He was truly the perfect man for me. I wasn't sure how I'd gotten so lucky, but I wasn't about to question it.

Thirty-Two

OUT ON THE GULF, the boat bobbed and swayed. It was enough to make those who didn't have their sea legs vomit, but I wasn't that person, and neither was Stu. The deck of the boat in the moonlight looked more gray than white as he lifted the black sack onto the edge of the boat.

I slit a line halfway down the bag, ripping into flesh as well. Her blood began to fill the bag, making me breathe a sigh of relief. If it had spilled into my boat, that meant extra cleaning I didn't want to deal with.

We pushed her over, hearing a "woosh" as her body hit the water. I tilted my head back, feeling the release of stress from my own body.

Stu stepped over and wrapped his arm around my waist, kissing my neck.

The true bliss we both felt at Katie's demise made me hopeful. I knew how dark I was inside; how dead I was inside. This kill made me realize how dead and dark Stu was inside, too.

I took Stu's face in my hands and kissed him.

"No one can stop us."

Acknowledgments

This book, let alone series, wouldn't be possible without the following people and references:

Practical Homicide Investigation (5th Edition) by way of a Thomas Harris acknowledgement. The FBI's *Serial Murder Multi-Disciplinary Perspectives for Investigators* Report (available free online), and *psychologytoday.com* for helping me add the necessary depth to Britney.

Ret. Sgt. Chuck Burns for his consultation where the textbook didn't answer specific questions.

Justin D., for helping me on ridiculously short notice with some nicknames.

Nathan, for his advice and invitations. I'm so very grateful I finally decided to take you up.

Mark…sweet Mark. Without you, I wouldn't be here. I love you more than I can express and always will.

Jason, for the awesome editing and blurbs and feedback and advice and just being you. You have made me the writer I am today. Let's not get arrested, please. At least not before we make that money.

Also by Amanda Byrd

13 Reasons for Murder:
Politeness Kills (#1)
Meathead (#2)
Philistines (#3)
Hungry (#4)
Bad Blood (#5)
Betrayal (#6)
Disillusioned (#7)
Harlot (#8)

The Morgan Davis Serials
The Girl at the Bottom of the Ocean (#1)
Before You Die (#2)

Serial Women of History
Amelia Earhart, Serial Killer *2024*

9 781734 371338